I0715763

ONCE UPON A TIME MACHINE

PEGGY GERBER

GLASS**SPIDER**PUBLISHING

Cover design by Judith S. Design & Creativity
www.judithsdesign.com
Published by Glass Spider Publishing
www.glassspiderpublishing.com

To all the people who clicked on my Facebook links, read my stories, and took the time to post a lovely comment. Those comments were this author's favorite gifts, and I thank you from the bottom of my heart.

Contents

Saving Aaron

My name is Maggie, and I am a murderer. As I sit in my jail cell awaiting indictment, I am in my own world, attempting to process my new identity as a killer. My hands are cuffed behind my back in preparation for my court appearance, but I'm not afraid. It will be very quick. When the judge asks for my plea, I have every intention of pleading guilty. The truth is, I am guilty, and I would do it again.

I committed the murder twenty-three years ago, but I had no memory of it until yesterday. I'm no expert, but that must be how time travel works.

The events that transpired to bring about this murder occurred on February 2, 2010. The day my family was shattered to pieces. On that day, my ten-year-old son, Aaron, got off the school bus and was struck and killed by a careless driver. The bus had on its flashing lights, but the driver of the car was so engrossed in texting that he didn't see Aaron until it was too late.

Aaron was hit so hard he flew twenty feet into the air before landing on his head.

My boy died alone, and it's my fault. For weeks, Aaron had been nagging me to allow him to walk home by himself. He kept begging, "Please, Mom, I'm not a baby anymore," and in a moment of weakness, I relented. If I had only been there, I could have stopped it.

The driver of the car, a seventeen-year-old boy named Kevin, was texting his girlfriend when the accident occurred. All it took was that one text message to snuff out my son's life and ruin an entire family.

When I arrived at the scene, the first thing I saw was a teenage boy sitting on the curb with his hands over his face, hunched over and sobbing. And then I spotted Aaron, and it was as if a huge vacuum had sucked all the air out of my lungs. He was lying on the ground in a pool of blood with his arms and legs twisted in unnatural ways. His beautiful blue eyes were open and vacant. My boy was dead.

I raced over and crouched down next to him, combing back his bloody hair, screaming for help, and sobbing into his ear, "Mommy's here, and Mommy loves you so much!" but he didn't hear me.

Frozen in a fog of unreality, I didn't know what to do. I threw my arms in the air, looked to the heavens, and began shrieking at the top of my voice, "No, God, no! Not my son! Not my Aaron!"

When it was time for the EMTs to take Aaron away, a police officer escorted me to his car, where I discovered Kevin's mother had arrived and shoved him into the back of the police car to prevent him from seeing what was going on. To block him from seeing the medics lifting Aaron's limp body onto a gurney and placing a sheet over his face.

There was a trial, and a lawsuit, but when it came time for sentencing, the judge was lenient. She took into account that Kevin was still a minor, as well as an honor student. It also helped his defense that his parents could afford a good lawyer. Kevin's punishment for killing my son was six months of community service, traveling to high schools around the state, and giving lectures on what can happen when you text and drive.

I was in the back of the courtroom the day the verdict was announced. I just sat with my mouth open in a silent scream as tears streamed down my face. I began to retch as I watched Kevin's parents embracing him and slapping him on the back. Their hearts were restored while mine was impossibly shattered even further.

The thing was, though, I would have thought it a fitting punishment if it had happened to someone else's child. It seemed almost fair, and Kevin was clearly devastated by what he had done.

Now I was just expected to go on with my life without my Aaron in it. After a year of closeting myself in the house, people told me it was time to move on.

I felt like the whole world was crazy and I was the only sane person in it. How could I move on when my Aaron was gone?

Aaron was such a great kid, everyone said so. He was smart and funny and at ten years old could already play the guitar so well he was the star of every school concert.

I used to love it when he asked me, "Mom, should I be a doctor or a rock star when I grow up?"

I would always put my arm around him and answer, "Honey, why not both?"

When I returned home from the courthouse, the silence in the house was deafening. For hours I paced around my house in a stupor. All I could think about was how it would be Kevin who would one day go to college, and it would be Kevin who would one day get married, and it would be Kevin who would give his parents the happiness I would never have.

Nobody can recover from the loss of a child, but some brave people take that loss and turn it into something positive. They find a way to go on. Not me. My broken heart put me into such a deep depression that nothing could diminish my pain.

For months, my husband Charlie nagged me, "Maggie, let's go

to counseling. Let's find a support group," but I just couldn't get off the couch, and I didn't want to. All I had left of Aaron was this pain in my heart, and I owed it to him to never give it up.

Charlie stuck around for a while, but eventually, he moved out. He said, "Maggie, you're draining the life out of me. I can't take it anymore." I don't really blame him. I know he loved Aaron too, that he was torn up as well, but he wanted to move on and have another baby. I only wanted Aaron.

After Charlie left, I arranged to work from home and only left the house to buy groceries. I was living my life as a ghost, and one by one, my family and friends gave up on me. Only my older brother stopped by once in a while.

As part of my routine, each night before bed, I watched an hour of world news. I liked to hear about all the awful things going on in the world, all the diseases, the earthquakes, the wars. It confirmed for me over and over how random life is, how unpredictable, and it made me feel a little bit less alone. I followed this routine robotically, without emotion, for twenty-three years.

Until that glorious night when there was a news story that caused me to jump up so quickly that I almost fell out of bed. A reporter was interviewing a team of brilliant PhD students at Princeton who were working on a time machine. My heart began beating so fast I had to sit right back down. This is what I had been waiting for. My depression suddenly lifted, as if a magician had waved a magic wand. I had a mission. Save Aaron.

It did not take me very long to find those Princeton students and arrange a meeting under the pretense of being an angel investor looking to fund their project. Little did I know that was exactly what I would become.

The team had put together a prototype of a time machine but lacked the funding to build a working model. The problem was the machine had a weird limitation that caused investors to turn it down. But not me. I had quite a bit of money from the lawsuit, and this was the perfect excuse to use it. Neither Charlie nor I had spent a penny of it—we saw it as blood money. I had enough to fund the entire project.

I gave it to the students with the understanding that I would be the first person to test the machine. We argued about it for months, the students moaning, "Maggie, there are serious safety issues," but they eventually gave in because they needed the money. I figured I had nothing to lose. If I died in the machine, it would be fine. I felt dead already. But if I succeeded, justice would be smiling.

It took close to a year after my investment for the time machine to be completed. I had no understanding of the mechanics of it, nor did I care. The machine's limitations were what concerned me. I would have seven seconds—only seven frenzied seconds—to complete my task once I was transported back in time. That was the excruciatingly short amount of time I would have in the time loop before being whisked back to the present.

I spent that entire year preparing for my trip. As we did not know the exact second my son was struck, seven seconds would not be enough time to stop him from getting off the bus, or stop him from crossing the street, or even telling my younger self to not let Aaron go to school that day.

The only thing I was certain would work was to murder Kevin the night before the accident. Seven seconds would be just enough time to pull a trigger and end the life of the boy who killed my Aaron. It would be a life for a life. How was that not fair? What mother wouldn't do that for her child?

I put together the perfect plan. I bought a gun and spent months perfecting my speed and my aim, going to the firing range every chance I got. I had always hated guns, hated violence, but I was driven by just one thought: *Save Aaron.*

When the time machine was ready, I rented out Kevin's former house for twenty-four hours. The owners asked questions, but I offered them ten thousand dollars to keep quiet, and they were happy to accept. You see, while the time machine had the remarkable ability to transport a person back in time, it could not take you to a new location. It was imperative that you were at the exact spot you needed to be.

Completely unaware of my murderous plan, the PhD students moved the time machine into Kevin's old bedroom. I knew exactly where to put it because I had briefly stalked Kevin's family after the accident. They had to get a restraining order.

With adrenaline shooting through my veins, all my senses were on high alert. We set the timer on the machine for February 2nd, three o'clock in the morning, twelve hours before the accident was to occur, and I stepped in. I would kill Kevin in his sleep. I had racked my brain for other solutions, but there was just no other way.

Seven seconds after the machine zapped me back in time, I returned to the present with a crushing headache, but my pain was transformed into ecstasy when I realized my plan had been a success. I now had a dual set of memories. While I still remembered every gruesome detail of Aaron's death and the twenty-three miserable years following, my brain exploded with twenty-three years of new, wonderful memories. I could remember how handsome Aaron looked at his prom, how our family rejoiced at Aaron's graduation from medical school, and then again at his wedding. The pride in his voice when he gushed, "Mom, I saved a patient's life today," and my new favorite memory, the look on Aaron's face the day his first child was born. How I treasure being a grandmother.

Along with the good memories, there were a few horribly sad

ones, as well. Especially the memory of that awful day twenty-three years earlier, when a neighborhood boy was murdered in his bedroom. A murder that, to this day, remains unsolved.

The boy's murder affected my family deeply, and I became a strong advocate for gun control, opening a local chapter of Mothers Against Gun Violence. Charlie and I came to realize how fragile life was, and we decided to have another baby. We named our little girl Kylee, after the young man who had died so tragically that night.

When I traveled back in time, I'd had to rent Kevin's old house from the family who owned it. But after returning from my brief seven-second trip, I found that I was now the homeowner. Charlie and I had bought the house from Kevin's family after the tragedy. His parents couldn't stand living there anymore, and we wanted to help them.

Looking around Kevin/Aaron's bedroom, I suddenly couldn't breathe. I had committed a murder in this room. I collapsed to the floor in agony of what I'd done, making a vow to dedicate the rest of my life to atone for my sins.

I am confident I will be convicted and sent to prison for my crime, and I want to be. After all, I turned myself in. I don't mind going to prison, and I won't have any regrets. I have twenty-three years of wonderful memories to cherish and replay in my head. But even though I was able to save my boy, it came at a huge price, and I don't want this to happen to anyone else.

So, I committed another crime.

The thing is, I am not being held on murder charges. Since Kevin never killed Aaron, there was never a lawsuit, and I never had the money to fund the time machine project. The team of students never found an investor, and the prototype was locked in a warehouse in Princeton, unfinished.

What I'm being held for is breaking and entering, as well as destruction of property. Shortly after my return, I drove to Princeton and destroyed their blasphemous prototype, trashing it repeatedly with a metal baseball bat. My family thinks I've gone insane, and I have no idea how to explain it to them.

You may wonder how seven seconds was enough time to pinpoint Kevin and murder him. Well, it wasn't. What I hadn't counted on that night was that Kevin's ten-year-old brother Kyle would be in the room instead. It was Kyle who died that night, but I still saved my Aaron, because on February 2nd, Kevin had a funeral to go to.

Necessary Exclusion

As the barbell-shaped spaceship entered the air space above New York City, Captain Xe2§ga yelled out, "Double check that the cloaking device is fully charged! It's been engaged since the Andromeda Galaxy, and we can't take a chance it will run out of power!"

"Are you talking to me, Captain?" asked Private First Class Gor§go.

"No, Private," thundered the captain, "I'm talking to my mother's big, hairy mole. Of course I'm talking to you! There are only two of us aboard this ship. Now stop asking dumb questions and go check the device."

Gor§go raced to the engine room with tears burning his oracles, wondering how he was going to last another six months with that oaf of a captain. When he arrived, he hit the control panel, checked the power grid, and gave the device an extra boost. Afterward, he approached the captain and timidly asked, "What's with the invisibility? Don't we want the aliens to know we're here? I thought we were recruiting new members for the United Interplanetary Union of Cooperation."

"For God's sake!" bellowed Caption Xe2§ga. "What have you been doing this whole voyage? Playing with your yang? Clearly, you haven't read the manifesto." The captain stamped his lower appendages. "This is a hostile planet, Private. We never go anywhere in the Milky Way galaxy uncloaked."

Gor§go bowed his three heads in apology.

"Private," the captain said, pointing to the computer screen, "study these images of Earth's dominant creatures, then set up the viewer scope and observe their activities."

"Yes, Captain," he replied. "Right away." After a careful analysis, Gor§go ambled to the scope, aimed his three oracles, and gasped. "Yikes! There are billions of them down there. They look like the roaches on the insect planet." He turned toward the captain. "These creatures only have one brain and are identical. Shall I document Earth as a planet of low-intelligence clones?"

"Private," huffed the captain, "you couldn't be more wrong. Earthlings are sentient beings that perform purposeful activities, and they're not clones. There are microscopic differences between each and every one. Look again, and don't jump to any more stupid conclusions."

Gor§go blew out a breath and thought about his mother's parting words. She told him to remember that Captain Xe2§a had a reputation for being extremely strict, but that he was brilliant, and it would be a great learning experience. She then gave him a bag of compliments and told him to eat one each time his feelings were hurt.

Gor§go retrieved his bag and rummaged through, deciding to eat the compliment reminding him he had graduated top of his academy. Feeling fortified, he returned to the scope, determined to find the differences between earthlings. Just when he was ready to give up, he spotted them. "Yes!" he shouted. "I am visualizing minor deviations in hues and sizes."

"Anything else?"

"No, Captain, I don't think so."

"Wrong again," groaned the captain. "Look here." He zoomed

in to maximum capacity. "Earthlings come in two varieties: fifty percent have a dink while the other fifty percent have a donk. They reproduce in pairs just like we do."

"Intriguing." Gor§go cocked his heads thoughtfully. "I wonder if these clone-like creatures can tell each other apart."

"Yes, Private. Despite the fact that they share 99.9 percent of their DNA, they are able to differentiate. Here's something interesting." The captain scratched his middle head. "The thing these beings most have in common is they love the very tiniest of the species. I find this baffling because those small creatures store their waste products in a bag wrapped around their bottom half."

"Eww," gasped Gor§go as he absently pinched close his nugunda. "How primitive." He gazed through the porthole. "What about leadership? Do they have a leader on this planet?"

"Great question, Private. They have many leaders, though the supreme ruler is an earthling they call Taylor Swift. When this commander is ready to share a message, thousands of worshippers all over the planet flock to stadiums. The leader then communicates with the minions by gyrating maniacally, and the minions gyrate back in response."

"Hmmm," Gor§go said. "Kind of like the insects." He narrowed his oracles. "Why would a planet with eight billion look-alikes be considered hostile?"

Captain Xe2§a shook his heads and muttered, "Private, I wish you had done your homework. What you are observing is only a small section of the planet. Swirl the scope around and you'll find your answer."

Gor§go slowly rotated the scope to the east and gasped. "Oh my God," he moaned. "The earthlings are blowing each other up." His cantaloupe-sized heart pounded as he recorded images for his report. "Why are they doing that, Captain? It's insane."

"It gets worse. Look here." The captain sighed and aimed the scope at a slaughterhouse.

Gor§go's four hairy appendages flew over his oracles. "I don't understand," he gulped. "The earthlings are murdering living beings for food. Why would they murder creatures on a planet with so much vegetation?"

The captain didn't respond but instead spun around and covered his faces with his tentacles. When Gor§go heard the sniffling sounds, his oracles opened wide. The captain was crying. Gor§go's minds began to race as he tried to process this new reality. Maybe the captain was not so different from him. He stood silently, heads bowed in respect, and whispered, "Take your time."

With his back still turned, the captain spoke softly, "We've been traveling to Earth for years, and we just don't know how to help them. Eighty years ago, during the most violent time in earthling history, we planted the idea for the United Nations. We even designed the building. Take a look, it's still there."

Gor§go admired the building with 5,400 windows.

Recovered from his emotional display, the captain dried his tears, turned around, and barked, "Private, I want you to take out your yang, and instead of playing games, do the research you should have done prior to coming here. Then write a full report for the UIUOC."

Gor§go strode off to his chamber quickly, chomping on the compliment reminding him that he was kind and considerate.

When the report was complete, Gor§go approached the captain and presented it to him.

"Read it out loud," said the captain.

Gor§go took a breath and began the summation. "At this juncture, Planet Earth must not be considered for inclusion in the United Interplanetary Union of Cooperation for the following reasons: The sentient beings on the planet have a penchant for violence, favor competition instead of cooperation, and hoard instead of sharing.

"It is my recommendation," Private Gor§go continued, "that we return to Earth in no less than eighty years to reevaluate the situation. By the way, Captain, I sent a message of peace to Taylor Swift. Hopefully, it will help this commander become a more effective leader."

"Great work," said the captain. "You finally got something right."

"Thanks, Captain," said Gor§go, and fed him the compliment. "It's brave to share your feelings."

The Mystical Rock

Annie shrieked as she hit the ground with a thud. She had been running for the bus when she tripped on an object, soared a foot into the air, and fell hard. Her floral skirt billowed around her head.

"Just my luck," she moaned.

Nothing in Annie's life had been going well lately. She hated her job, nobody would publish her book, and after two years of trying, she wasn't able to get pregnant. It was no wonder her depression was creeping back in. The only good thing she had in her life right now was her husband, Jacob. But lately, their relationship had been strained due to all the tension in the house.

Annie's face flushed crimson as she sat on the ground and began to assess her injuries. She had fallen very hard on her hands and expected one or both of her wrists to be broken. The last time she fell like this, she was in a cast for six weeks.

She began flexing her wrists and examining her knees for injuries, wondering why there was no pain. Other than ripped pantyhose, a couple of light scratches on her hands, and a bruised ego, she felt completely fine.

She stood up slowly and began searching for the object that had tripped her. When she looked down, she spotted a rock the size of a grape, smooth and black, with a beautiful, intricately designed Hamsa painted on it. She picked it up and examined it with a feeling of growing awe. The ornamental hand was painted a rich-blue color with delicate swirls of purple and specks of gold glitter. She thought it was one of the most beautiful works of art she had ever seen.

Annie knew exactly what this symbol meant because her mother often wore a Hamsa necklace for good luck. She owned one in every color and size. She believed the symbol represented the hand of God and would ward off the evil eye. She often tried to convince Annie to wear one. She said it might help with some of her struggles.

Annie always groaned and rolled her eyes at her. Unlike her mother, Annie was not superstitious. But there was no denying there was something special about the rock. She carefully wiped off the dirt, placed it in her pocket, and continued on to work. It fleetingly crossed her mind that perhaps it was the rock that had saved her from harm. Then she shook her head and laughed at herself.

Tiptoeing into her office almost an hour late, still flexing her wrists, Annie prepared herself for the inevitable lecture from her boss. As she walked in, her friend Kristy jumped up to meet her with a big grin on her face. "Today's your lucky day," she said. "Mr. Jenkins just called and said he was having car trouble, so he won't be in until the afternoon."

Annie sighed with relief and did a little happy dance as she settled into her workstation. All morning long, she kept sneaking peaks at the beautiful rock and wondering about it.

When it was time for lunch, Kristy met Annie at her desk, and they walked to the cafeteria together. As Annie described her eventful morning, she pulled the rock out of her pocket and placed it in Kristy's hands. "Isn't this the most gorgeous Hamsa you've ever seen?" she exclaimed. "The artist is amazing. I don't know how anyone could have painted such an intricate design on such a small rock."

Kristy rolled the rock back and forth in her hands. "I'm confused. It just looks like a plain black rock."

Annie frowned. "That's not funny. You're making me sound crazy, and you know I'm sensitive about that."

Kristy gently placed her hands on Annie's shoulders. "I would never make fun of you. I swear, all I see is a black rock."

At the lunch table, Annie passed the rock around to her coworkers and asked what they saw. They all agreed there was nothing special about the rock and asked Annie if she was feeling okay. Kristy tried to make a joke about the whole thing, suggesting that perhaps the rock was like that dress that had been posted to Facebook a couple of years back. Although most people saw the dress as blue, some saw it as gold.

After a very bewildering day, Annie walked home from the bus wondering if she was having hallucinations. She figured either her luck was about to change, or she was becoming unhinged. As she walked past the local convenience store, she impulsively went inside and bought a lottery ticket, immediately pulling out a coin to scratch off the numbers. She pumped her fist in the air when she realized she'd won fifty dollars. It was the first time she had ever won anything, and she celebrated by picking up Chinese food for dinner.

When she arrived home, Annie put the food in the oven to warm and opened her computer to check her email. Her heart began to pound when she saw an email from an agent, and her hands shook as she clicked it open. As she read the message, her breath caught in her throat. The agent loved Annie's book and wanted to represent her. Her book would be published. Tears began flowing down Annie's face as she re-read the email five more times.

As soon as Jacob walked through the door, Annie jumped into his arms and began sobbing. She asked him to pinch her to make sure she wasn't dreaming. After telling him all about her weird, wonderful day, she tentatively put the rock in his hand and asked what he saw. She closed her eyes and hoped he saw the same thing she did.

He shook his head. "Annie, all I see is a black rock, but I believe you, and I've always believed in you. I'm so happy for your good news."

The next day, Annie bought a special little acrylic box to keep the rock in and carried it with her wherever she went. Her luck continued to grow, and pretty soon she was getting acceptances for many of her previously rejected short stories. Six months later, she was posing for the camera as she proudly held her first published book in her hands. When the book began to get good reviews, it gave her the confidence she needed to quit her job and become a full-time author. The ideas for her next book were flowing freely, and her old writer's block was a thing of the past. Every morning, Annie woke up looking forward to the day, and without her even realizing it, her depression faded away. Annie felt genuinely happy.

It was about a year after finding the rock that Annie and Jacob made plans to meet for dinner at their favorite restaurant to celebrate their tenth anniversary. Annie arrived first, and the hostess seated her by the window. Soon after, Jacob walked in carrying a dozen roses. Annie's face lit up when she spotted him.

As he joined her at the table, he took her hands in his and said, "Annie, we have had such a wonderful year. I'm so proud of you and how well your new career is going. I love you so much. Let's go crazy and order the most expensive bottle of champagne in the restaurant."

"Thanks, honey, I love you too," Annie said, "but I will not be drinking for at least another seven months."

They made a toast to their wonderful news with a bottle of grape juice and discussed all the events of the past year.

"I owe everything to my good luck rock," she told Jacob. "It completely changed my life. My book got published, I haven't felt depressed in a very long time, and the best news of all, we're expecting a baby. How else could you explain it? It had to be the rock."

"Annie," Jacob said, "you sent query letters to like a thousand agents, and your book is wonderful. You're a very talented writer. I always said sooner or later, some agent is going to be smart enough to represent you. That's not luck, that's hard work and talent."

Annie furrowed her brows. "Well, how do you explain my depression getting better? I had been feeling awful for such a long time."

"You went to a therapist for a year. You practice meditation, you write in a gratitude journal, and you've worked so hard doing all the exercises your therapist gave you. You need to give yourself credit for feeling better."

Annie sighed. "Okay, here's the biggest thing. We've been trying to get pregnant for two years now, and it's finally happened. How do you explain that? It has to be due to the luck of the rock, doesn't it?"

"Honey," Jacob said, "you'd been so stressed for such a long time. You're finally relaxed now, maybe your body is smart enough to know that now is the right time to have a baby."

On the ride home, Annie thought about everything Jacob had said. It made a lot of sense, but there was still one huge unanswered question. Why was she the only one who could see the Hamsa on the rock? That had to mean something, didn't it?

A week after their anniversary dinner, Annie and Jacob went to the radiology center for her first ultrasound. As usual, Annie had the rock in her purse and touched it for reassurance while they awaited their turn. Looking around the office, she noticed a little girl about five years old sitting on her mother's lap clutching a pink teddy bear. The little girl appeared sickly and was resting her head on her mother's shoulder. Annie looked at the little girl's mother and saw tears in her eyes.

Annie impulsively jumped up and approached the little girl. "Hi," she said, "my name is Annie. What's yours?"

The little girl smiled and said, "Hi, my name is Jasmine, and this is my teddy bear. Her name is Jasmine too."

Jasmine's mom smiled at Annie, grateful for the distraction.

"Do you want to see something super cool?" Annie asked Jasmine.

The little girl brightened. "Yeah, I want to see something super cool!"

Annie put the rock in Jasmine's fragile hand and asked, "What do you see?"

Jasmine's face lit up. "Mommy, look at the beautiful orange butterfly! It's just like the one we saw at the park last week. Isn't it so pretty? Can I keep it?"

Annie turned to Jasmine's mom. "Can you see the butterfly as well?"

The woman wrinkled her nose. "Of course."

To her amazement, Annie could not only no longer see the butterfly, but she couldn't see the Hamsa, either. All she saw was a plain black rock. Now she knew for sure that this rock was meant for Jasmine.

She told Jasmine's mother, "This rock will bring you good luck, but you must promise to take good care of it. I don't understand why or how it works, but it does. Bring it with you to all of Jasmine's doctor appointments."

Although she appeared skeptical, she and Jasmine promised to take good care of it. Annie felt confident they would keep their pledge and walked away with a spring in her step.

A few minutes later, Jacob and Annie clasped hands as they followed the technician to the ultrasound room. They waved goodbye to Jasmine, who was busy showing the butterfly to Jasmine the bear.

Annie beamed, "I just know the rock was meant for her. I'm ready to make my own luck now."

A year later, as baby Amalia was napping in her crib, Annie began work on her newest novel. She already had a title for it: *The Mystical Rock.*

The Pet from Outer Space

Rosie was deep into REM sleep when a deafening thud jarred her awake. She jumped out of bed, her heart pounding like a jackhammer, and raced to the window to investigate. As she peered through the glass, she rubbed her eyes in confusion. She couldn't believe what she was seeing. Sitting in the middle of her tomato garden was a glowing cigar-shaped spaceship. Just like the ones in the movies.

Abandoning her usual common sense, Rosie threw on her robe and slippers and wandered outside. At first she hovered motionlessly by her back door, but after a few minutes took a few cautious steps toward the ship.

As she got closer, she suddenly became aware of a clicking noise coming from inside. She jumped a foot in the air and gasped. She stood rooted to the spot as the hatch began to slowly open, inch by inch, until a life form peeped through.

Rosie's mouth dropped open as she watched the most handsome man she had ever seen climb out. What a hunk! Shoulder-length, scraggly auburn hair, cobalt-blue eyes, and a perfectly chiseled body, which she could clearly see because he was naked.

The alien creature jumped off the ship and turned his head to look around. As soon as he spotted Rosie, he began waving enthusiastically and moving in her direction. When he stood directly in front of her, Rosie froze like a statue, unable to breathe. After a few seconds, her well-ingrained good manners kicked in and she held out her hand in greeting.

"Hi…I-I'm Rosie," she stammered.

The handsome man flashed Rosie a dazzling smile. "Hi, I'm Bobo."

He took her hand in his and licked it. As she dried her hand on her robe, Rosie noticed he was wearing what looked like a dog collar around his neck.

Her face a mask of confusion, Rosie took Bobo's hand and brought him into her house. He glowed with excitement as he began touching every object in sight, picking up all her knickknacks and turning them over in his hands.

While Bobo kept himself entertained, Rosie raced into her father's room and plucked out a pair of pants and a shirt for him to wear. She couldn't possibly concentrate on anything while he was naked.

She held out the clothes to him, and he furrowed his brows. He didn't know what to do with them. Rosie motioned how to put them on, and he followed her lead.

As he dressed, Rosie put her hands over her face and wondered if she was having a psychotic break. At thirty-five years old, she had spent the last five years in this isolated farmhouse caring for her sick father and had often felt desperately lonely. Now that her dad had passed, she found herself sinking into a depression.

Slowly, Rosie uncovered her face and saw Bobo was still there, and he was still smiling. She looked into his beautiful eyes and was suddenly overcome by the most inexplicable feeling. She felt as if a magnetic bond had formed between them—and just like that, she was willing to risk everything to help him. She briefly pondered if this was what love at first sight felt like. She'd never thought it could happen to her.

As the gravity of the situation began to set in, Rosie realized that the spaceship had probably been picked up on radar and that federal agents would be arriving at her home soon to investigate the crash. She would have to figure out some way to hide Bobo, or at least disguise him.

Rosie went into her kitchen, put up a pot of coffee to help her think, and pushed Bobo into a chair at the table. When the brew was ready, she poured herself a cup and guzzled it down. Then she poured another and set out two plates of doughnuts. She looked Bobo in the eyes and declared, "I want to help you, but first, I need some answers."

Rosie took the seat next to Bobo and stared at him. Her mind was a jumble of questions, and she didn't know where to begin. Finally, she blurted out the first thing that came to mind. "Why are you wearing a collar? Are you a slave?"

Bobo frowned. "A slave, no. I'm a pet. A most beloved pet."

Rosie sucked in a breath. "So someone does own you?"

"No. Well, technically, yes. But it's not like anybody orders me around. I am Keeper's pet, and It loves me and takes great care of me."

Rosie's eyes opened wide as she barked, "What do you mean, It takes care of you?"

"Well," said Bobo, "Keeper supplies everything I need and brings me along on all of Its space missions. It's not like It forces me to come. I want to. I enjoy being on the ship and learning about the universe. I like being a pet." He beamed at Rosie, and his eyes lit up. One of the things I especially enjoy is that each night before bed, Keeper rubs my back and shoulders with Its eight green furry tentacles. Sometimes on these missions, I must carry heavy boxes, and the massage really gets the knots out."

Rosie pictured being touched by eight green furry tentacles and shuddered. Trying to get back on track, she asked, "So how long have you been with Keeper?"

"Keeper adopted me when I was about eight years old, and we've been together ever since." Bobo looked at Rosie's neck and frowned. "Why don't you have a collar? I'm sorry, are you a stray?" He took a bite of his doughnut and moaned, "Mmmm, what is this thing I'm eating? It is the most delicious food I've ever tasted."

Rosie tried hard to ignore the fact that Bobo was eating the doughnut with his feet and felt grateful she'd given him her father's pants. Rosie took the uneaten doughnut off her plate and placed it in Bobo's hands, demonstrating a more polite way to eat food. When she was sure he had the hang of it, she continued her questioning. "Where is Keeper now?"

Bobo's eyes began to tear up. "Keeper died on the spaceship. Keeper was very old, and this was to be Its last mission. Fortunately, Keeper taught me how to navigate the ship, so I was able to land it myself." He began to sob. "Now I'm all alone."

Rosie got up and wrapped her arms around him. Her heart sped up as she felt his strong, solid muscles underneath her father's shirt. It took everything she had to regain her focus, but she knew if she was going to make Bobo appear somewhat normal before the authorities came, she would need to work quickly.

Questions began shooting out of her mouth like bullets. "Bobo, where are you from? Are you human? How do you speak English? Why were you naked? Do you have a wife? Could you demonstrate how Keeper rubs your back?"

Rosie sat back down, and Bobo walked behind her. He placed his hands on her shoulders, tears still flowing down his face. "I know I can't do this as well as Keeper because I only have two hands, and they are not furry, but I'll try my best."

Gently, he began to massage her neck and shoulders, and Rosie let out a deep sigh of satisfaction.

As Bobo's hands trailed down her back, he began to answer her questions. "I come from Home, where else would I be from?" He took a deep breath, momentarily lost in thought, and continued. "Yes, I am human. Marriage is only for Keepers, and English is the language that all pets speak. Oh, and I was naked because pets don't wear pieces of cloth. By the way, they are very uncomfortable. Can I take them off?"

Rosie absently shook her head. "Maybe later."

Bobo stood in front of Rosie and frowned. "Who takes care of you? Where is your Keeper? Is all the food on this planet as delicious as this…what did you call it? A doughnut?"

Rosie raised her hands to Bobo's neck and gently began removing his collar. She explained to him that if he wanted to stay, he would have to follow her instructions. She told Bobo, "On this planet, humans are their own keepers. But if you like, we can be each other's keeper, and this could be your new home."

A smile lit up Bobo's face as he exclaimed, "Yes, I would be delighted to live here with you!"

Rosie's heart leapt, and for the first time in a very long time, she felt excited.

As she expected, not long after Bobo's arrival, two government agents appeared at her door. Rosie sent Bobo to the bedroom and told him to stay there until she called him. She invited the agents inside, and they began drilling her with questions. First and foremost, they wanted to know if Rosie knew why they were there.

Rosie played dumb. "Of course. You must be here because of that glowy thing in the backyard. I know I should have called someone when I first saw it, but I was too petrified to do anything."

Then she swore under penalty of imprisonment that she hadn't spoken to anybody about the object. The agents confiscated her phone and computer just to make sure.

After Rosie answered what seemed like a million questions, she went to her bedroom, put her arm around Bobo's shoulder, and introduced him to the agents.

"This is my fiancé, Bob." She crossed her fingers behind her back and added, "As you can see, my poor fiancé is horribly shaken up by this incident. He's having a massive anxiety attack. He can't possibly answer any questions today. You'll have to come back at a much later date if you want to speak with him."

The agents took one look at Bobo's tear-stained face, unkempt hair, and ill-fitting clothes and agreed it would be best if they came back in a few days. Meanwhile, they would be posting a guard outside Rosie's door to make sure nobody left the house until the object in the backyard was removed. They would be keeping her phone and computer, as well.

After the agents had finished documenting Rosie's statements, they turned to Bobo. "Okay, Bob, take care of yourself and try to relax. We'll see you again in a couple of days."

"Actually," Bobo began to say, "you pronounce my name Bo—" but before he could finish, Rosie cut him off and told him to go to the kitchen and get another doughnut, explaining to the agents that food helped calm him down. Bobo skipped off with a smile. He really loved the food on this planet.

As they put away their notepads, Rosie stifled a grin and ushered the agents out the door. She walked back into her house with a spring in her step, her loneliness melting away like ice cream on a hot summer's day.

"Bobo, I'm back," she called out and headed into the kitchen.

She knew it wouldn't be easy teaching Bobo how to act like an earthling, but she was up for the challenge.

True Love's Kiss (or Not)

Snow White's eyes flew open wide as she bolted upright in her glass casket. "What do you think you're doing?" she hissed at Prince Charming. "Have you been living under a rock? You can't just kiss a woman without her permission! For God's sake, haven't you ever heard of the Me Too movement?"

Upon seeing her awake, the seven dwarfs whooped with joy and raced to Snow White's side to help her out of the casket.

As they took her hands to assist her, they scowled at Prince Charming, who stumbled backward and stammered, "But...but...but...that was true love's kiss! I am Prince Charming, your hero, who has come to take you away to be my wife. I love you!"

"First of all," sneered Snow White, "that was not true love's kiss. That was breath so bad it actually woke the dead. Secondly, you say you love me just because I'm pretty? What about my personality? What about my hopes and dreams? What about what I want?" Snow White stared into the prince's eyes. "No, thanks. I decline your offer of marriage." She spun around and began walking toward her cottage in the woods.

Prince Charming chased after her, shouting, "What do you mean what about what you want? What about what I want? I am a future king, and I demand that you become my wife!" He began to pout. "How can you turn down the offer to be my queen?"

Snow White shook her head and sighed. "Men," she muttered under her breath. "I already have seven, I don't need one more."

As a last-ditch effort to win her over, the prince grabbed Snow White's wrist and made a solemn promise. "Marry me, Snow, and I will get revenge on your wicked stepmother. I will cut off her head on the day of our wedding."

"Ewww!" said the seven dwarfs as they shuddered in disgust.

Snow White glared at the prince. "I don't need your help. I already have a plan. My wicked stepmother is growing older every day. I figure in about five years, her magic-looking glass will tell her there are loads of women fairer than she is. She won't be able to stand it. She'll storm off to a faraway land, and I will become the rightful queen. My father was a king, I am a princess, and one day, I will rule over my kingdom with kindness and compassion. That will be my revenge."

Prince Charming, not accustomed to being treated in such a way, climbed onto his horse and shot Snow White a look of contempt.

As he rode away, Snow White took a deep breath, turned to Grumpy, and laughed. "Is that a smile I see on your face?" She then wrapped her arms around her seven friends and said, "Let's go home."

The Girl Who Barked

"Honey, stop the car!" Holly shouted. "I hear a baby crying."

Danny dutifully pulled the car over even though he hadn't heard a thing. He was really worried about his wife. They had recently made the decision to stop pursuing fertility treatments, and Holly was taking it hard. They were embarking on this road trip to clear their minds and begin the healing process.

As soon as they came to a stop, Holly jumped out and cocked her head to hear better. She ran into a wooded area by the side of the road and began spinning in circles, trying to determine from which direction the faint sound was coming. She called to her husband, who was standing by the car, frozen like a statue.

"Danny, help me find the baby!"

"Honey, please," he pleaded, "get back in the car. I think you're imagining it."

"No!" shouted Holly. "I'm not crazy. I hear a baby crying."

She began racing through the woods, stumbling on tree roots, zigzagging back and forth, furiously trying to locate where the cries were coming from. Danny watched by the side of the road, tears stinging his eyes, sure his wife was having some sort of mental breakdown.

Just as he summoned the courage to drag her back to the car, Holly screamed, "Honey, come quickly!"

Hidden in the hollow of a tree was a brand-new baby girl with golden hair and cerulean eyes. She was wrapped in a pink blanket. A note was pinned to the blanket, which Holly read out loud. "Dear Holly, please take care of my baby girl. I'm counting on you."

The note was signed *Kala*. As soon as Holly finished reading the note, it burst into flames. Holly dropped the ball of fire and watched as the burned particles gently floated to the ground.

Shaking his head in disbelief, Danny asked, "What just happened?"

With a smile spreading across her face, Holly gushed, "Our prayers were answered."

Danny stood with his mouth hanging open, unable to speak. When he finally found his voice, all he could think to say was, "Uh, Holly...we don't even have a car seat."

Holly whipped out her phone, googled the nearest Baby-Mart, and hopped into the backseat of the car, cradling the infant in her arms. They soon arrived at the store, where they bought all the supplies they would need to travel with a baby and headed straight home.

They spent the entire return trip discussing how they would present this to their families. They decided the best thing to do was to say Holly had been pregnant all along but was too nervous to tell anybody because of her past miscarriages. Everyone believed them.

They named the baby Mikaela, and right from the start, they knew there was something different about her. She was a fussy baby, and Holly spent hours each day bouncing her, pacing back and forth, singing lullaby after lullaby, trying anything to soothe her.

Each night, Holly would drop into bed exhausted, and

sometimes just as she was drifting off, she could swear she heard barking.

Mikaela hit the terrible twos with a vengeance; almost anything could incite a tantrum. It was just after her second birthday, as Holly was trying to soothe a particularly bad episode, that she realized she was embracing a dog.

Holly screamed and shook so badly that she almost dropped the small puppy. She didn't know what to do. Her precious baby girl had transformed into a tiny golden retriever.

Holly collapsed on the couch and began to gently pet Mikaela, her mind racing to come up with a logical explanation. By the time Danny arrived home, Mikaela had transformed back into a toddler. Holly met her husband at the door and broke into sobs as she told him the story, knowing he would think she was losing it. He didn't.

"I knew something weird would happen one day," Danny said, "but holy cow, Holly, this is a humdinger."

He went into the kitchen and brewed a fresh pot of coffee before sitting down at his desk. He popped open his computer and spent the entire night scouring the Internet looking for an answer. By the morning, he knew.

With his stomach in knots, Danny tiptoed into the bedroom and gently shook his wife awake. He put his arms around her. "Our Mikaela is a metamorph."

Holly bolted upright and furrowed her brows. "Mikaela is a *what?*"

"A metamorph," whispered Danny. "A shapeshifter."

Holly's eyes flew open. "You mean like those aliens on *Star Trek*? Is Mikaela an alien?"

"No," Danny sighed. "She's actually from Scotland, a sparsely inhabited island off the northern coast." He took a breath. "We had always hoped to understand a little bit more about Mikaela's birth, and now we know. Her mother must have been a meta-morph as well."

Holly dropped back down on her pillow and put her hands over her face. She had a lot to think about.

Danny called in sick that day and went to see his brother who knew how to access websites few others could find. The two siblings spent the morning researching metamorphs and discovered the name of a shaman who professed to be an expert. Holly called him immediately and pleaded for an emergency appointment. Then they packed up the car and drove twelve hours to meet him.

By the time they knocked on Dr. Jamison's door, both Holly and Danny were exhausted and terrified. The doctor met them at the entrance and took Mikaela out of her mother's arms. He escorted them into an examination doom and gently placed the toddler on the table.

It didn't take long to confirm the diagnosis. Mikaela was indeed a metamorph, although in her case, she was a mixed-race one. Evidence indicated that while one parent was a metamorph, the other was a human. That explained why she could shapeshift only into a dog.

The doctor asked Holly questions about Mikaela's temperament, explaining that there were both good and bad metamorphs. He declared that based on her difficult infancy and toddlerhood, Mikaela was a bad one.

Holly's ears began to burn. She looked directly into Dr. Jamison's eyes and began stomping her foot. "No!" she bellowed. "Dr. Jamison, you are a fraud. My Mikaela is good!" She stormed out of the doctor's office clutching Mikaela in one hand and pulling Danny by the collar with the other.

Over the next few years, Holly devoted herself to helping Mikaela deal with her temper. She discovered that relaxation was key to preventing transformations. Holly studied meditation and deep breathing and poured every ounce of her heart and soul into helping her daughter. Nobody was going to tell her that her little girl was bad.

After a while, Holly became an expert at predicting Mikaela's moods, and when she detected a foul one coming on, she would take her daughter's hands and say, "Kalee, let's practice our breathing."

As Mikaela grew older, Holly taught her many different relaxation techniques, and by the time Mikaela was six, she could fully control her transformations. As soon as she felt a fit coming on, she would turn on some music, close her eyes, and practice breathing just like her mother taught her.

That's not to say Mikaela never had a lapse. Sometimes, when she didn't get her way, she would transform into a dog and sit in the corner and growl. She knew her parents hated it, and she did it to irritate them.

When Mikaela turned seven, Holly enrolled her at the local elementary school, confident she was ready, and for the first few months, everything went smoothly. Mikaela loved school and made her first real friend, a little girl named Sara.

One day, as the two of them were sitting on swings in the schoolyard, the class bully came up to Sara and called her ugly. Mikaela clenched her fists, jumped off the swing, and bit the bully in the leg so hard he needed stitches.

The lunch aide grabbed Mikaela by the arm and dragged her to the principal's office. When Holly arrived at the school to pick her up, Mikaela looked at her mother and grinned, "Mommy, I didn't transform."

Mikaela was suspended for the rest of the year, and the doctors could not figure out why the boy's wounds looked like a dog bite.

On her twelfth birthday, Mikaela woke up to the smell of blueberry pancakes wafting into her bedroom. She jumped out of bed and raced downstairs, excited for pancakes and presents. She had been campaigning for an iPhone, and as she opened her last gift, her face fell. She hadn't gotten one. She looked at her parents and grumbled, "I'm protesting. I am going to transform into a dog and stay that way until I get that phone."

Holly shrugged her shoulders. "Okay, Kalee, that's fine, turn into a dog. See if I care. But it's Saturday, and I'm visiting Grandma at the nursing home, and you're coming with me. You can't stay home with Daddy this time." She put a leash on the now mid-size golden retriever and dragged her out of the house. Too stubborn to transform back, Mikaela let her mother lead the way.

When they arrived at the nursing home, they went straight to the memory care unit where Holly's mother lived.

"Hi, Mom," Holly said, "I have a special surprise for you today. I brought our dog."

Holly's mom, who was often agitated and combative on visiting day, began petting the dog and calmed down immediately. She looked into the dog's eyes and said, "Kaylee, is that you?"

Mikaela climbed into her grandmother's lap and began licking her face. The three of them spent a wonderful afternoon together, and Holly's mom was more interactive than she had been in months. It was that afternoon that Mikaela discovered she had a special gift for easing the emotional pain of others.

Over the years Mikaela volunteered at her grandmother's nursing home as well as the local group home for autistic children, sometimes as herself and sometimes as her alter ego. When she graduated school as a psychiatric nurse, nobody was prouder than Holly, who felt grateful every day for the gift of Mikaela.

On the night of Mikaela's graduation, Holly had a vivid dream.

A beautiful woman came to her and said, "Thank you for taking such good care of Mikaela and always believing in her."

A single tear leaked out of Holly's eye as she whispered back, "Thanks for choosing me."

The Golden Death Pact

"I have to be honest with you, Claire, no matter how carefully I manage your money, you and John are going to outlive your savings within the next few years."

Claire's eyes burned with tears as she sat motionless, trying to process the information her financial adviser was giving her. She was having trouble accepting what he was saying. How could it be? She and John had saved for years for their retirement. They were looking forward to a long and happy life together.

She turned to Mike. "What exactly do you mean?"

"Look," Mike said, turning his computer in Claire's direction. "You and John have about $273,000 saved in your combined retirement accounts. Your money hasn't grown in a long time. The markets have been in a slump for years, and the interest rates are at their lowest. I'm sorry, Claire, it's not just you. Nobody has been making money lately."

Claire looked Mike in the eyes and pleaded, "Tell me we'll be okay. You can figure out a budget. Right?"

Mike sighed deeply as he pulled a chart out of his folder. He handed it to Claire. "It's just not enough. With the development of the diabetes-busting drug Quidapess and the improvement in statins, the average lifespan has increased to one hundred and eight years. Some people are even living into their one hundred and twenties. You and John will potentially need income for the next thirty-eight years." He took a breath. "Look at what's happening with Social Security. The system is strained to the max. Benefits were cut in half in 2035, and now, just a year later, they're about to be cut again. If you don't have enough savings, you're in deep trouble."

Claire put her hands over her face and whispered, "What are we supposed to do? John was recently laid off, and I've been unemployed for a while. Nobody will hire us at our age. I'm getting really scared."

Mike scribbled a few things on his notepad and turned to face Claire. "Well," he said, "you do have a few options. You have two extra bedrooms in your house. You could rent them out to boarders."

Claire's eyes flew open. "No," she stammered, "not going to happen."

"You could sell your house, pay off your mortgage, and move in with your children. Or you could ask your children for money."

"That's a hard no," barked Claire. "John and I would never burden our children like that. Besides, they need to save for their own retirement."

Mike steepled his fingers and spent the next few minutes deep in thought. He then opened his desk drawer, took out a large envelope, and handed it to Claire.

With his voice beginning to quiver, Mike said, "I'm not recommending this, and please know I have no vested interest. I'm just presenting this as an option for you and John to not have to live in poverty."

Claire furrowed her brows, confused as to why Mike was getting anxious. She pulled the stack of papers out of the envelope and read the title page of the document: Medicare Gold for Special Seniors. She was immediately intrigued. As she continued reading what appeared to be a government-issued contract, her hands flew over her mouth.

"Are you kidding me, Mike? This is a death pact!" she bellowed. Her jaw began to clench as she continued. "Explain this to me in plain English. It's written in legalese, but it looks to me like a death pact with the government. Please tell me I'm not right."

Mike put his head down. "Well, technically, I guess it is, but don't write it off until you hear all the details. If you sign this contract, for the next twelve years you'll never have to worry about money again. All you'll have to think about is how to live your best life."

Claire took her purse off the back of her chair and took out two ibuprofen tablets. Her head was beginning to pound, and she knew she would need a clear mind to fully understand the contract. She swallowed the tablets with a glass of water, handed Mike the empty glass, and ordered him to continue.

"I'm going to break it down for you," Mike said. "Step one: You sign a contract agreeing to end your life the day after your eighty-second birthday. Two witnesses and a notary will be present. Step two: Uncle Sam tacks a large monthly stipend onto your Social Security payments, and you stop worrying about money. Step three: You and John go on a nice vacation or buy gifts for the grandkids or do whatever you want with the money."

Claire sat in stunned silence, hanging on to Mike's every word. "Go on. The document is twenty pages long. It must say a lot more than that?"

"Yes, it does," Mike continued. "Step four: You move into government-subsidized housing. It's not mandatory, but if you're interested, you would live in a luxury building with a doorman, a gym, a pool, and many other amenities. It's quite nice."

Claire raised her eyebrows to indicate she wanted to hear more.

"Step five," Mike said, "and the best part, you would receive Medicare Gold. Each and every one of your medical expenses would be met, including prescription drugs, dental care, hearing aids, and loads of other things. You'd never have to worry about medical bills again."

"What about John?" Claire asked. "Would he have to sign it too?"

"Well," said Mike, "if John signs the contract as well, he'll receive the same benefits as you. If not, he could move into the luxury apartment with you, but he would lose all his Social Security and Medicare benefits. He would be at your mercy for medical and living expenses. You'd have to pay out of your pocket for everything for him."

"And what happens if we take the subsidy, and then on our eighty-second birthdays, we change our minds?"

Mike said, "Well, Claire, you'd be convicted of fraud against the government. You'd spend the rest of your life in prison."

For the next two hours, Claire and Mike worked together to calculate how long her savings would last with every different kind of budget. In the best-case scenario, Claire and John would run out of money in five years.

Claire began to whimper, "John and I are both seventy years old. If we're going to live past a hundred, we'll be living in poverty for so many years." She picked up the contract again. "Twelve great years," she muttered under her breath, "or thirty horrible ones. Twelve years of traveling and enjoying life, or thirty years of living in poverty."

She smiled momentarily as she pictured herself and John taking Caribbean cruises and European vacations and not having to stress about medical bills. John was scheduled to have a hip replacement soon, and they had been worrying about their co-pays. Her smile quickly turned to a frown when she pictured herself and John living in a one-room apartment and having to take money from their kids.

"How do they do it, Mike?" she asked.

Mike knew exactly what she meant. She didn't have to spell it out. He whispered, "They give you a pill. It's entirely painless. Afterward, they'll pay all your funeral expenses. There'll be no financial burden for your children."

Claire shook her head as she picked up the envelope full of papers. "Okay, Mike, I understand. Let me speak to John, and I'll get back to you."

"Take all the time you need," he said, "but just remember, the sooner you sign the contract, the more money you'll receive."

Claire stood up and groaned in pain. She had been sitting for over two hours, and every part of her was stiff. As she stretched out her aching body, she mumbled to herself, "Who the heck wants to live to be one hundred and eight years old, anyway?"

Lost in her thoughts, she silently put on her jacket and walked to the door. She turned to face Mike and waved goodbye. "We'll talk soon."

As she began walking to her car, she pulled out her phone and called her husband.

"John," she said, "let's meet at the diner for lunch. We have a lot to talk about. Oh, and make an appointment with Bill. We're going to need some documents notarized."

Inside NASA's Hidden Files

Despite the harsh weather conditions and extreme temperatures, scientists have long speculated that years ago, life existed on Venus. Evidence was mounting that Venus, often referred to as Earth's twin, was once alive with oceans and forests and fluffy white clouds floating in an atmosphere of oxygen and nitrogen—until, little by little, the greenhouse effect warmed the planet and destroyed every aspect of life.

To confirm this scientific hypothesis, NASA sent a space rover to Venus to dig underground and transmit pictures back to Earth. The photos showed millions of bones and teeth. And they were all human.

The Doll That Saved Christmas

Chloe huddled in her closet pretending to be invisible. Her parents were fighting again, and she clamped her hands over her ears to block out the sounds of vases and lamps crashing against the living room walls.

Her father was lashing out in a drunken stupor, screaming and cursing as her mother cowered in a corner. Chloe had always been terrified when her parents fought, but this time was worse. This time, it was her fault. Why did she have to beg her mother to buy a Christmas tree when she knew it was against her father's wishes?

As the fear built up inside her, seven-year-old Chloe came up with a plan. She decided she would hide out in her neighbor Hildy's apartment until it was safe to go home. Hildy had always been kind to her and her mom, and sometimes when her dad wasn't around, she and her mother would join Hildy for tea and cookies. It was their little secret because her dad had forbidden them from going to her apartment. He said there was something very strange about that woman, and he didn't like her.

Chloe emerged from her closet, took a deep breath, and crept silently across the living room floor, praying her father wouldn't see her. She opened the door as quietly as she could, and when she got outside, she looked to see Hildy standing above her with open arms. Chloe fell into her hug and burst into tears. Hildy didn't have to ask what happened. She could hear the screaming echoing throughout the hallway.

She brought Chloe into her kitchen where there was a cup of hot chocolate and a plate of her favorite cookies waiting at the table. Chloe sat down and began poking at the marshmallows floating in her cup, wondering how Hildy knew she would be coming.

When she asked, Hildy just smiled and said, "I'll be right back. I have to let your mom know that you're here. Don't worry, honey. Everything will be okay. I promise."

Hildy ambled across the hall and knocked on her neighbor's door. Chloe's dad, Frank, yanked it open and growled, "What do you want?"

Hildy calmly explained, "Chloe is at my house having a little snack, and I won't bring her home until everyone has calmed down."

"Who do you think you are to tell me how to raise my kid, you batty old witch?" Frank sneered.

"Oh, I'm just a friendly neighbor who knows how to dial 911 and Child Protective Services."

Frank spat on the floor and slammed the door in her face.

When Hildy returned to her apartment, she found Chloe standing by the bookcase staring at one of the dolls in her collection. It was her most treasured doll, and she took it off the shelf and gently placed it in Chloe's arms. "Chloe, meet Felicity."

Chloe had been instantly drawn to this exotic doll and sang a little lullaby as she lovingly cradled her soft, warm body in her arms. She began to stroke Felicity's long raven hair and ran her fingers over the tiny beads intricately woven into her brown suede dress. When she looked into Felicity's beautiful round face, she was mesmerized by shining porcelain eyes as blue as the ocean.

Hildy winked at the doll, then put her hands on Chloe's shoulders. "Felicity has always been a very good friend to me, but today she has chosen you as her best friend. Before she becomes yours, though, you must promise to take very good care of her."

Chloe's face lit up as she made a solemn vow.

That night, Chloe took Felicity to bed with her and felt relaxed for the first time in weeks. There was something about the doll that made her feel calm. She snuggled Felicity close to her body and was just drifting off when her dad stomped into her room. He snatched Felicity out of her arms and roared, "I said no gifts this year! Especially not from that nosy-body witch next door!"

As the tears began streaming down Chloe's face, two savage red lights beamed out of Felicity's eyes and bore into Frank's, temporarily blinding him. The doll whispered menacingly, "How did you like being blind? If you dare to frighten my girl again, I will burn the eyes right out of your head."

Frank's hands began to shake, and he dropped Felicity on the floor like she was on fire. He ordered Chloe to throw the devil doll out the window. Chloe began to whimper as she slowly got out of bed and picked Felicity up, remembering her promise to always take good care of her.

For the first time in her life, she defied her father and brought the doll back to bed with her. When Frank realized what she was doing, his mouth twisted into a snarl, and he slapped her across the face. He had never hit her before, and Chloe cried out from shock as much as pain.

Hearing the commotion, Chloe's mother raced into the room just in time to witness the abomination. Suddenly, every ounce of fear she had ever felt toward her husband evaporated. "Frank," she bellowed, "get out of my house now or I'm calling the police!"

Frank scowled and stomped out the door in a rage, too angry to speak.

That night was Christmas Eve. Chloe's mom gave her the exact gift she had been wishing for. Together, they packed their bags and moved in with Chloe's grandparents.

The next morning, Chloe awoke to the aroma of freshly baked Christmas cookies wafting through the air. She climbed out of bed a little disoriented, gathered Felicity in her arms for courage, and walked down the stairs looking for her mother.

When she heard her mom's voice, she followed it into the living room where she saw all her cousins sitting around the Christmas tree laughing and opening presents. Her family shouted, "Merry Christmas, Chloe!" and like magic, her heart grew wings, and she began laughing too. She winked at Felicity, gave her a big hug, and joined her cousins around the tree.

What's a Grandma?

Nine-year-old Ariel burst into the house, practically knocking the screen door off its hinges. "Mommy, Mommy, Mommy!" she bellowed.

Lauren, quite used to Hurricane Ariel, looked at her daughter and laughed. "What is it this time, honey?"

Ariel threw down her backpack and jumped into her mother's arms, panting. "Today in school when my friend Harrison asked our teacher what a grandma is, her face got red as a tomato and she yelled, 'Go home and ask your mother, and don't ever ask that question again!' I never saw my teacher get angry before, it was really scary." Ariel sniffed and took a deep breath, looking into her mother's eyes. "So, Mommy, what's a grandma?"

Lauren could feel the hot acid bubbling up in her throat as she began to hyperventilate. Although she'd known this day was coming, she was not ready. How could she ever be prepared to steal away the innocence of her only daughter, knowing it would change her life forever? Just like it had hers when she was nine.

For the next few minutes, Lauren paced the floor, taking deep breaths and wrestling with this gut-wrenching question as Ariel watched her wordlessly. When she finally made a decision, Lauren wrapped her daughter in a bear hug. "Ariel, you're a big girl now, and I think you're ready for the truth."

Ariel furrowed her brows as her mother took her hand and

brought her into the kitchen. Lauren made them each a cup of hot chocolate and placed three cookies on a plate in front of Ariel. Ariel's eyes opened wide with delight, and she became giddy. She hardly ever got junk food.

As she took her first small nibbles, savoring each bite, she wondered once again why her parents never ate junk food and why grown-ups always wanted to talk about boring things like the best way to grow organic vegetables, or which vitamins to take.

Sitting at the kitchen table, watching her daughter enjoying the cookies, Lauren became hypnotized by the swirling steam rising from Ariel's cup. It transported her back to the day she'd had this same talk with her own mother. The day her panic disorder had been born.

Ariel looked at her dazed mother and cried, "Mommy, what is it, already?"

Jolted back to reality, Lauren watched as her daughter dunked her cookie into her hot chocolate, laughing and smacking her lips in delight, oblivious to the serious turn this conversation was about to take.

Readying herself for the task, Lauren sat up straight and plastered a fake smile on her face. "Ariel, what I'm about to tell you is an important part of our history, but you must promise not to tell your friends."

Ariel nodded her head in earnest, and Lauren began.

"In the year 2041, a great virus swept through the earth. It was called Novo-41, and it was the most contagious virus man had ever known. It infected people all over the world, but the truly awful thing about it is that it killed everybody over the age of eighty instantly. We were at the complete mercy of this virus."

Ariel's eyes opened wide. "People used to live to be in their eighties? That's crazy." Gesticulating wildly, she knocked over her cup of hot chocolate, splashing it all over her new shirt, as well as the table and the floor.

Tears came to Ariel's eyes, but Lauren said, "Don't worry, honey, that's what mops and washboards are for."

Lauren grabbed a mop and a bucket of water as she passed some towels to Ariel. As they cleaned up the mess, Lauren said, "Honey, believe it or not, some people even lived to be over a hundred."

Ariel's face was a mask of shock as Lauren continued.

"The virus mutated and mutated again, eventually killing off all people over seventy, then sixty, then fifty, and within a year of the first reported case, there wasn't a single person in the world who wasn't infected. This virus embedded itself into the very fabric of our DNA. What that means is that now, even babies are born with the virus. Do you know what DNA is?"

"Of course, Mommy, I *am* in third grade!" Ariel began to absentmindedly twirl her ponytail. "I know I have blond hair because you have blond hair."

"That's right, and Grandma had blond hair too. So let's answer your question. A grandma is your mommy's mother and your daddy's mother, and a grandpa is your mommy's father and your daddy's father. Do you understand?"

Ariel began jumping up and down. "Of course! You're saying I have two grandmas and two grandpas? Where are they? When can I see them?"

Lauren gulped back tears. "I'm so sorry, honey, but all four of your grandparents have died. People don't live long enough to become grandparents anymore. It's just around the time that a person's hair begins to turn gray that the inborn virus begins to exert its effects."

Ariel shook her head in disbelief. "You mean a person's hair can turn a different color?"

"Yes, it can, or at least it did. I know this is going to sound scary, but first I want you to understand, it doesn't hurt. To put it simply, the virus consumes the thinking part of a person's brain. At first, people begin seeing things out of the corner of their eye, but then, little by little, they develop hallucinations. Eventually, people can no longer tell the difference between what's real and what isn't."

Lauren could see that Ariel needed a break from this serious conversation and sent her upstairs to change out of her wet shirt. As Ariel walked to her room, her brain was a swirl of confused thoughts and questions. She mechanically changed her clothes and returned to the kitchen.

"Mommy, what happens to people when they start seeing things?" Ariel whispered.

Lauren began forcefully scrubbing Ariel's shirt against the washboard, taking out all her anger and frustration on the block of wood as she prepared to answer Ariel's question. After a moment of hesitation, she continued.

"I'm proud to say that we take very good care of our elders. As soon as people have their first vision, they move into a special home called Hospice Heaven." Lauren crossed her fingers behind her back as she added, "It's such a happy place because people get to live together and make so many friends."

Tears burned Lauren's eyes as she recalled the day she'd brought her own mother to Hospice Heaven. She'd had to drag her mother into the building kicking and screaming, and it took everything she had not to put her mother back into the carriage and have the horses take them home. Deep in thought, Lauren absently stared at the floor and picked at her cuticles, forgetting that her daughter was waiting for answers.

She returned to the present when she heard her daughter

whimpering, "Mommy, are you okay?" Ariel had never seen her mother so worried before, and it terrified her.

Lauren smiled at her daughter and said, "I'm okay, honey, because it's a happy story. When people first arrive at Heaven, they have jobs and fun things to do, and we can visit them all we want. But as they get sicker, the visits stop, and they get to relax like they're on vacation. The thing to remember is that every single person at Heaven is treated with kindness and compassion. We're all in this together."

Lauren took her daughter's hand and brought her outside. The sun warmed their faces as Lauren hung Ariel's shirt on the clothesline and took a breath of fresh air. As Ariel walked off to the barn to visit the horses, Lauren used the time to organize her thoughts. One day she would tell Ariel that in the past not everyone lived on a farm, but today was not the day for that.

When Ariel returned, they went to peek at the vegetable garden. The seeds had been planted and the tiny buds, green and full of promise, were just peeping above the surface. On a normal day, it would have brought happiness to Lauren's heart, but today it brought only sadness. The budding plants only served to remind her of the budding terror in her mother's eyes the day she'd had her first vision. Lauren was only eighteen, and she wasn't ready to say goodbye to her mother. But as sad as Lauren felt now, she was also happy she could finally share memories of her beloved mother with Ariel.

After a few minutes, Lauren signaled for Ariel to sit on the porch while she sprinted into the house and retrieved some old photo albums.

For the next two hours, mother and daughter laughed and cried as they looked at pictures of all of Ariel's grandparents, each one having written a special letter for the grandchild they would never know. Lauren would one day do that too, for Ariel's children.

When they finished reading all the letters, Lauren gave Ariel a book her grandmother had written for her. It was called *Grandma's Watching Over You with Love*.

Although Ariel was old enough to read it herself, Lauren scooped her up onto her lap and read it to her. Together, they mourned a life that they would never have.

Later that night, as Lauren tucked her daughter into bed, Ariel checked her mother's hair for gray—something she would do every night from then on—and asked the question Lauren had been dreading. "Mommy, will you and Daddy go to Heaven too?"

Lauren sat down on Ariel's bed and began stroking her hair. "Yes, Ariel, but I promise Daddy and I will make sure you're ready. And don't forget the most important part. You won't be alone because of Match Day. You know that's how Daddy and I met. The year you turn eighteen, the town mayor will match you up with a very nice young man, and you'll get married. You'll share Wedding Day with all of your friends your age. Isn't that wonderful? It'll be one of the happiest days of your life."

Lauren prayed her lie was convincing because it was important for Ariel to have something special to look forward to. Then she closed her eyes and vividly recalled how scared she'd been on her own Match Day.

As she lay in bed staring at the ceiling, Ariel felt a world of sadness fill her up, and she began to cry. "Mommy, what am I going to do without you? Why did this terrible virus have to happen?"

Lauren wiped her daughter's eyes. "Don't you see, Ariel? This virus is a gift. It taught us to slow down, respect the Earth, and return to a simple way of living. We took a wonderful step backward and are healing the earth. Now, when we look at the night sky, we can see thousands of stars twinkling up above. It's like they're saying thank you for your help. Our planet has been re-stored."

She kissed Ariel goodnight.

"But the best part is, because we know our time on earth is limited, we understand how precious life is. We never forget to tell the people we love how much we love them, and we don't get mad at each other for silly things like spilling hot chocolate. So, while some things about the virus are sad, the world is a much happier place because of it."

And even as the words came out of Lauren's mouth, she was still trying to convince herself.

Magical Cowboy Boots

Last night, I dreamed that I killed my neighbor's dog. That I snuck into the yard next door and slipped a little poison into King Kong's water bowl. I'm not a monster, but it was the third time that week the annoying beast's earsplitting howls crept into my dreams and woke me up before sunrise. The sleep deprivation was killing me. Too agitated to go back to sleep, I dragged myself out of bed and went to the kitchen to make a pot of coffee. By the time my husband joined me, I was so grouchy I instigated a fight.

"Erica," Michael grumbled, "stop picking on me. This is your anxiety talking. Why don't you make an emergency appointment with your therapist? This stress isn't good for you."

Tears burned my eyes as I contemplated his suggestion. I wished Michael could understand how embarrassing my mental health issues were to me, and how I already didn't feel normal. I ended up storming out of the house without saying goodbye and stomping my way to the bus stop. Of course, just when I got there, a speeding car drove through a puddle and splashed muddy water all over my brand-new beige coat. I should have gone home to change, but I was so ashamed of how badly I'd treated Michael that I waited in that filthy coat for a bus that never came. I ended up having to take an Uber to work, which cost me half a day's pay.

When I arrived at the office, my boss came running over before

I even had a chance to hang up my coat. He told me it was my day to mentor Beverly. Again. It seemed like it was always my turn. The fact was, Beverly went to the pub for lunch every day, and nobody else would work with her. Some days, her boozy breath was so strong it left me with a headache.

It was one of those days. To make matters worse, at exactly four o'clock, Bev yelled to me, "Goodbye, Erica!" and she walked out the door with her friends while I had to stay an extra two hours unsnarling her computer and correcting all her mistakes. It was so unfair; my boss refused to acknowledge the situation and treated me like a doormat.

When I was finally done correcting Boozy Bev's work, everyone in the office had already gone home and I was all alone. I shut down my computer and dragged myself to the elevator, which of course had just broken down. By the time I walked down the twelve flights, I was panting and so upset that I knew I'd need to work off some of the adrenaline before going home. Michael hated it when I walked in agitated like that, and I was sure he would tell me to quit my job. The last thing I wanted was to start another fight.

When I got to the gym, I went straight to the locker room to change. After stuffing my purse in a locker, I opened my gym bag to pull out my workout clothes and realized I'd left my sneakers underneath my desk at work. Instead of panicking, I spent the next few minutes taking slow, deep breaths and was able to calm down. I would still be able to take a yoga class.

Still breathing deeply, I dressed, shoved my gym bag into my locker, and tossed my snow boots on top. Everybody did that. The lockers were too small for any items that couldn't be compressed.

After leaving the locker room, I headed off to do some relaxing yoga, but when I got to the room, there was another surprise. It seemed that the entirety of the continental United States was taking a yoga class that day. The room was so crowded that I had to shove myself into a tiny crevice in the back of the room. After ten minutes of trying to do downward dog standing up, I left the class and trudged back to the locker room to get dressed.

The first thing I noticed when I walked in was that my boots were no longer on top of my locker. In its place were some used tissues and a pair of dirty socks. My fists clenched as I quickly threw on my clothes and began searching for my boots. I ran down row after row of lockers in a frenzy, looking on the floor, in the bathroom, and on the feet of every woman in the locker room. By the time I got to the front desk, tears were burning my eyes.

"My boots have been stolen," I moaned to the desk clerk. "Please help me."

Barely looking up from her phone, the clerk calmly replied, "I'm sorry for your loss, ma'am, but there is nothing we can do. We don't keep extra boots lying around, and as your contract states, we're not responsible for your personal property."

Tears began to spill over as I pleaded with her. "It's twenty degrees outside, and there's snow on the ground. You must have something I could put on my feet."

The clerk furrowed her brows, deep in thought, and smiled. "Yes, yes, I do have something." She went into the back and came out with a pair of flip-flops. My eyes flew open wide in shock as she began to sneer. "Look, I'm really sorry, but that's the best I can do. You can either call a cab or try the thrift store down the block."

I grudgingly put on the flip-flops and slammed the door as I left. I looked down at my bare feet, zippered my coat up to my throat, and ran to the thrift store as fast as I could. I slipped and slid on the ice the whole way. By the time I arrived, I was shivering and could no longer feel my toes.

When I tried pushing open the thrift shop door, I discovered it was locked. I wasn't sure I could handle any more disappointment. I knocked on the window, and a middle-aged woman wearing a peasant blouse and a long-fringed skirt came rushing over and opened the door. She took one look at my blue feet and gasped, "Oh my gosh, what happened?"

She put her arm around me like a kindly grandmother and escorted me to the couch at the back of the store. As I peeled off my jacket, she told me to make myself at home, and that she'd be right back. A few minutes later, she returned with a pair of woolen socks and a cup of herbal tea.

For a moment, it crossed my mind that maybe she was my guardian angel. As I sat there sipping the hot tea, I began to sob, and the story of my bad day poured out. The store owner shook her head in sympathy and pointed to a sign that read *Miss Clarice will tell your fortune. Only ten dollars.*

I shook my head. "No thanks, I don't believe in that stuff."

"What's your name, honey?" she asked.

"Erica," I replied as I pulled a tissue out of my purse and blew my nose.

Clarice grinned at me. "You know what, Erica? I like you, and you've had an awful day. I'll do the reading for free."

I thought what the heck, my day can't get any worse, so I sat back, smiled, and said, "Okay."

Before I knew what was happening, Clarice grabbed my hands and shut her eyes. She began swaying back and forth and chanting in some foreign language I'd never heard of. After a few minutes, she dropped my hands, looked me straight in the eye, and crooned, "Today is your lucky day, Erica. The first day of your new life! I see a long vacation in store for you, as well as a career change. You and your husband will soon renew your vows. You will be happier than you've ever been."

I couldn't help but roll my eyes at how ridiculous that prophecy sounded. After five years of marriage, Michael and I were having a lot of problems. It was more likely we would end up in divorce court than renew our vows.

After the reading, Clarice walked over to the shelf where she kept the boots. She studied them very carefully before pulling off a pair of brown leather cowboy boots. She hugged them to her heart before handing them to me.

"These boots are very special. They have the power to bring you good luck, but you must believe in them. I have a strong feeling they are meant for you." She winked and added, "And I'm hardly ever wrong. Wear them for good luck, and when you no longer need them, pass them on to somebody else."

I smiled in gratitude and slipped the cowboy boots on my feet. They were not really my style, but they were warm and a perfect fit. I wasn't sure how Clarice knew my size, but everything about her was weird.

When I stood up, I rocked back on my heels and began admiring the boots. They were growing on me, and I started to think about how cute they would look with a pair of jeans or a denim skirt.

I paid Clarice twenty dollars for the boots and waved enthusiastically as I walked out the door. I was still chuckling at the thought of magic boots as I began crossing the street. I never saw the car coming.

When I woke up in the hospital, Michael was holding my hand and Clarice was sitting on a chair in the corner. My husband told me I had a shattered femur, a broken wrist, and a bad concussion. I lay there in shock for a long time without speaking. My leg and wrist were throbbing, and I was dopey from the medication. I couldn't figure out what Clarice was doing in my room.

When Michael left to buy some coffee, I looked at Clarice and began to wail, "What are you doing here? Why would you tell me the boots would bring me good luck? This has been the worst day of my life."

Clarice walked over slowly and sat on the edge of my bed. She began combing my hair back with her fingers just like my mother used to do, taking care not to press too hard. She looked at me with her big green eyes and said, "Don't you see, Erica? This was a great day. It was the day you didn't die. The first day of your new life."

Then she kissed me on the cheek and disappeared out of my life like a ghost.

It would be weeks later that I asked Michael why he'd let a stranger into my hospital room that first night. After all, he didn't know Clarice.

"Honey," he said, "what are you talking about? It was just the two of us."

After the hospital discharged me, I went to rehab, where I spent the next few weeks learning how to walk again. The physical therapist told me I might have a permanent limp. Afterward, Michael and I took a cross-country vacation and renewed our vows in Vegas. The accident made us realize how much we meant to each other, and we wanted to rededicate our love.

I never went back to my old job. Being in rehab had given me the opportunity to work on my mental health as well as my physical health, and I developed some tools to keep my anxiety under control.

I finally understood that mental health is just health, and anxiety is nothing to be ashamed of. With a new sense of confidence, I decided to enroll in nursing school. I had always dreamed of becoming a nurse, but I was never brave enough.

As for the magic cowboy boots, I still wear them, but I don't really need them anymore. I'm almost ready to pass them on. They've already worked their magic.

Suspended in Time

After forty long years of nothingness in suspended animation, Eliana blinked open her eyes. Slowly, her muddled thoughts began to clear, and she put her hands together in a silent prayer of thanks.

Eliana and the two thousand crew members aboard the Aurora 1 had traveled millions of miles to Galina, an Earth-like planet. Their plan was to make the planet habitable for the thousands of people that would begin arriving in two years. Earth was getting overcrowded, and the elite demanded more space.

As a veterinarian with special expertise in freezing and defrosting embryos, Eliana's job would be to bring to life the thousands of animal embryos they brought with them. The International Space Alliance had had its eye on Eliana for years and was determined to do whatever it took to get her on board.

When they first approached her about the mission, she declined. She told them she wasn't willing to abandon her family, no matter what the compensation. Desperate to have her, the Alliance agreed to reserve a spot for her family on the Aurora 2.

For the first few months on Galina, Eliana was so busy she barely had time to breathe. She spent all her days and most of her nights in the lab, incubating embryos and ensuring conditions were right for successful births. As the months flew by and healthy animal babies began to arrive, Eliana was finally able to relax.

On the morning of her birthday, Eliana woke up in a funk. She was missing her family so badly that her whole body ached. Tears stung her eyes when she thought about her kids, and how if she were home, they would be serving her breakfast in bed right now. They always made her feel special on her birthday. With depression weighing down on her like a suit of armor, Eliana lay in bed sulking and ruminating. Just when she felt at her lowest, her friend, Juliet, burst through her door singing, "Happy Birthday."

"Ellie," Juliet laughed, "you don't look a day over seventy-nine."

"Hey!" Eliana snapped playfully. "That's not funny. You know very well I'm only forty."

"Technically, you're eighty. You were born in 2071, and now it's 2151. Do the math."

Eliana grimaced. "Maybe instead of bombarding me with bad jokes, you could stay with me to watch videos of my kids. My boys are teenagers now, but I love watching them as toddlers." She sniffled. "I can't wait for them to join me in fourteen months. It's killing me that I will have missed two years of their lives." She looked down at the floor. "Sometimes I wish I hadn't come."

Juliet shrugged her shoulders. "So why did you? I wouldn't have come if I had anyone back home."

"Ethan talked me into it. He said I'd be crazy to turn down the opportunity. He told me the two years would fly by." She sighed heavily. "I'm not really mad at him. He knew I would love my job here, and I do. Just yesterday, I liberated another twenty cows from their incubators, and they're healthy and beautiful. In less than two years, we'll have our first fresh milk on Galina!" She touched Juliet's hand, pouting. "But sometimes I get very lonely here. Please stay. I could really use the company."

Juliet turned to Eliana and grinned. "I have a surprise for you.

I was just at the control center checking incoming messages, and there's a video from Earth that just arrived."

And just like that, Eliana's depression transformed into joy as she pumped her fist and shouted "Yes! The perfect birthday gift. Can you transfer the file to my computer?"

"Already done. There's more good news. It's a VR interactive series 212.2, so it'll be like your guests are actually in the room with you. You can ask or say anything, and an algorithm will match their prerecorded responses with whatever you've said. Pretty great, huh? It's a huge file. Clearly, someone has a lot to tell you." Juliet left, waving goodbye to her friend, relieved to see Ellie was feeling better.

As soon as she was gone, Eliana opened her computer and clicked on the video with a rush of anticipation. When the images appeared, she furrowed her brows in confusion. Who were these people? She cocked her head to take a closer look and narrowed her eyes. There was something familiar about this eighty-year-old man and his two gray-haired companions.

As the realization suddenly hit her, Eliana clutched her chest and collapsed onto her bed. Her breath came in gulps, and her body began to tremble. She covered her face with her hands and moaned, "This can't be true…this can't be true! Please, God, make this not true!"

Very slowly, Eliana removed her hands from her face. Her biggest fear had become a reality. The old man was her husband. And the gray-haired men were her sons.

Eliana sat in stunned silence, trying to process what she was seeing and having difficulty organizing her thoughts. When she finally found her voice, she shrieked, "Oh, my God, Ethan! What happened?"

"Hi, sweetheart," Ethan replied. "I know you must be shocked.

As you can see, we never got on the Aurora 2."

Eliana jumped up and began pacing the floor in circles, her heart racing like a cheetah as she screamed, "Ethan, how could you do this to me? We had a plan! You were scheduled to come in two years. We were going to be a family again!"

Ethan looked at his wife and whispered, "I'm so sorry, Ellie. We were packed and ready to go, but on the day of departure, Hunter wasn't feeling well. He had a fever, and they wouldn't let him board the ship. I couldn't leave him behind, and I know you wouldn't have wanted me to. I tried to rebook the flight, but the next one available wasn't for ten years. By that time, the boys didn't want to go. Their life was here, on Earth, and we were happy." Ethan dropped his eyes. "After I remarried, it was no longer an option."

Eliana's face turned crimson as she picked up her coffee mug and hurled it at her husband's head. The cup flew through his image and shattered against the wall, brown liquid dripping down in streaks. Eliana dropped back onto her bed and bellowed, "You did *what?* You got remarried? What's wrong with you?" She attempted to take some deep breaths but couldn't get her breathing under control. Gasping for air, she turned to look at her sons. "Tyler, Hunter. Is that really you? You're so old! How could you grow up without me?"

"I'm sorry, Mom," Hunter said. "It was really hard after you left. We missed you so much. We struggled for a long time, but we want you to know we're okay now. Please don't hate Dad. He didn't remarry for twelve years. He's been a good father."

Tyler spoke up next. "Mom, I have a special birthday surprise for you. My son, Levi—your oldest grandson—is on the Aurora 12. He'll arrive on Galina in about thirty-nine years. You will be with family again."

Eliana's eyes flew open. "Thirty-nine years! I'll be almost eighty. An old woman."

"Please be happy, Mom," Tyler said. "Levi can't wait to meet you. We've told him all about you. I know you'll be a wonderful grandmother to him."

Eliana put her hands on her head and began wailing.

Ethan whispered, "Okay, Ellie, I want you to stop the video now so you can begin to process everything. Watch the video a little at a time. Hunter and Tyler have worked very hard to make it special for you. They'll tell you all about their work and their families, and you'll get to see your grandchildren. You'll be so proud."

Eliana gulped. "Ethan, will you be sending more transmissions?"

Ethan shook his head. "Sorry, Ellie, this will be the only one. We saved for years to be able to do this for you. Happy birthday, sweetheart. We miss you, and we'll love you forever."

Eliana slammed her computer shut and lay on her bed in the fetal position, tears soaking her pillow.

Juliet tiptoed in and put her arms around Eliana. "I stuck around when I heard you crying," she said. "I'm so sorry, Ellie. Take all the time you need to mourn. When you're ready, we'll meet your grandchildren."

Visiting Grandma

Outside, a fierce wind blows as the temperature plummets inside the drafty old house. Grandma sits in her rocking chair as Emily lovingly wraps a shawl around her skeletal shoulders.

Sipping a cup of tea, Emily turns to her grandmother and says, "Tell me again, Grandma. How did you die?"

The Cake with the Secret Ingredient

Ariel's heart was racing like a roller coaster when she stumbled into the coffee shop. As she turned her head from side to side searching for her sister, the heavenly scent of the freshly baked pastries made her mouth water. When she spotted her younger sibling, she joined her at her table. "Thanks for meeting me here, Julia. Did you order anything yet?"

"Yeah, I ordered you a slice of triple-layer chocolate cake with buttercream frosting and shaved chocolate on top, and I ordered myself the strawberry shortcake with extra cream and fresh strawberries. Also, cappuccinos for both of us."

"Thanks," Ariel muttered. "But listen, I have something to tell you."

Before she could continue, the waitress arrived with their food, and Julia dug immediately into her strawberry shortcake, moaning with satisfaction.

Ariel shook her head. "Julia, I think you and your cake should get a room!"

"Ha-ha, Ariel. Laugh all you want, but this is the most delicious thing I've ever tasted. The Bakerians just keep outdoing themselves. Think about it. They came to this planet, brought us new medicines, and then they gave us food so good there are no words to describe it. And how about the fact that it doesn't make you gain any weight? It's like a miracle. I eat cake every single day now, and I don't worry about my weight. I'm so happy. Aren't you?"

Ariel sighed. "I was happy, but now…"

Julia cut her off. "Remember when the Bakerians first arrived? We were so scared. We were sure we were going to die. I still gasp every time I see them. I mean, their lizard-like appearance and creepy yellow eyes are terrifying. But they learned our language, and they were gentle, and they turned out to be a gift to our whole planet. They said they came here to help us, and they kept to their word."

"It's not true," Ariel hissed. "They didn't come here to help us."

Julia stopped eating and gasped as her sister was racked with sobs.

"Julia," Ariel said, "what I'm about to tell you is really scary, and you must keep it a secret until I can figure it out."

Julia stuck out her finger and the sisters pinky-swore, just as they had when they were children.

"You know how I've been eating a lot of cake?" Ariel said. "It's like I'm addicted or something. I can't stop myself. Well, a weird thing is happening to me, and I don't know what to do. I need your help."

The color drained from Julia's face as she grabbed her sister's hand. "What's wrong?" she nearly stammered.

Ariel leaned in and lowered her voice. "Today, when I went to the bathroom, I pooped green. Not forest green. Not dark green. Fluorescent green. Like those glow necklaces you get at weddings and bar mitzvahs."

"Oh, my God, Ariel! That's gross."

"There's more. I didn't know what to do, so I asked Zac for his help. He told me to cut it open and see what was inside. So, I did…and there were eggs inside. Thousands of them. They were wiggling like they were about to hatch."

Julia scrunched her face in disgust. "Zac told you to fish your poop out of the toilet and you did it? Disgusting! And then you cut it up? What's wrong with you?"

Ariel sighed. "Focus, Julia, you're missing the point. The fact is, there are eggs in the cake. I think the Bakerians are giving us this cake so we can incubate their eggs and have the alien babies hatch in the sewers. I'll bet the reason we never gain weight from the cake is because the eggs are sucking out the nutrients from our bodies and storing them as their own food. You know how the Bakerians provided tons of cake and distributed it all over the world? We were all so happy. Nobody would have to go hungry anymore. Well, they're still baking and delivering cakes every single day. There might be millions of people pooping out eggs. What are we going to do?"

"I'm so confused!" Julia cried. "Why is this happening to you and not to me? I love cake too."

Ariel's face fell. "I'm so ashamed. Zac and I have been eating cake for all our meals and snacks. Lemon chiffon cake for breakfast, apple cake for lunch, and carrot cake with soft, cream cheese frosting for dinner. We figured since the cakes had fruits and vegetables baked inside, they were okay for meals. After dinner, Zac and I would have chocolate cake for dessert. We're so addicted we can't stop eating it! Even after my discovery, I still had cake for lunch, and I'm about to eat the chocolate cake in front of me now."

Julia furrowed her eyebrows suspiciously. "Why isn't this on the news, or all over the internet?" When she spotted her sister pulling her plate closer to her, she cried, "Ariel, get your hands away from the cake. Don't even think about touching it!"

Ariel's breathing became ragged as she fought the impulse to eat the cake. She interlocked her fingers so she couldn't pick up her fork. "Zac and I think it might be some kind of conspiracy. The government has to know what's going on, right?" She paused for a moment and continued. "I don't know why only some people seem to incubate the babies. Maybe it's people with a certain blood type. I spent the whole afternoon doing research, and every time an Instagram post or tweet appeared, it disappeared instantly. I think some alien force is sucking it off the internet as soon as it's posted. I've never been so scared in my life."

She unfurled her fingers and picked up her fork, but Julia's eyes flew open and she cried, "You've got to be kidding me!"

She slapped the fork out of Ariel's hands and dumped the cake on the floor. When Ariel bent down to pick it up, Julia slapped her hands again.

"Stop!" she screamed. "We have to tell Mom. Mom will know what to do. We'll lock you in a room at her house and you'll stay there until it's out of your system. We'll take care of you and make sure you don't eat any more cake. We'll break this addiction. We'll do whatever it takes. I promise."

Ariel thought about what that would mean. No more banana fudge cake with chocolate chips and walnuts for breakfast. No more pineapple upside-down cake for lunch. No more double chocolate brownie cake for dessert. Ever again.

Her mind was becoming cloudy. She was having trouble think-ing. Her thoughts were jumbled as she flashed on all the different varieties of cakes she had eaten over the past few weeks. The crav-ings were becoming unbearable. She couldn't give up her cake.

"Julia, please don't tell anybody!" she exclaimed. "I'll handle this myself. Zac and I will figure it out. Promise me you won't tell Mom."

Julia's legs buckled as she got up from her chair. She had never seen her sister this desperate. "We need to leave right now," she exclaimed. "Let's go." Trembling, she grabbed her sister's arm and held on tightly. "We're going to Mom's. It'll be okay. You will be okay. You have to trust me."

Arm in arm, the sisters exited the bakery and turned in the direction of their mom's house. As they began walking down the street, Ariel suddenly became aware of a scream piercing the air. She looked around to see where it had come from and realized it had come from her mouth. While in a deep frenzy, she had taken a knife from the coffee shop and stabbed Julia in the stomach.

Ariel dropped to her knees and held her moaning sister in her arms. "I'm so sorry," she said. "I love you, but I must have cake."

She let go of her sister's limp body and began to wail, horrified at what she had done. She wished she were the one bleeding. She got up, dialed 911, and ran away as fast as she could. She didn't know where she would go or what she would do, but she knew she had to have cake.

Stopping to catch her breath, Ariel looked down at the hands that had betrayed her and saw they were covered with her sister's blood. It was not red.

My Year with a Witch: Excerpts from the Diary of Grace Hildegard Lawrence

March 2, 2023

Dear Diary,

Screw you! The last thing I ever wanted to do was write down my problems in a diary and re-live the event, but my therapist said if I don't start doing my assignments, I'll never get better. She made my mother cry. So here it is. My name is Gracie, I'm nineteen years old, and I can't leave the house by myself. I spend my days sitting in my room, eating Froot Loops straight from the box and binge-watching movies about teenagers with cancer. There's actually quite a lot of them. My diagnosis is agoraphobia, PTSD, anxiety, depression, and survivor's guilt. Quite an impressive quintet, if I do say so myself. Anyway, since it's just Mom and me, and Mom has to go to work, she decided I would go next door to Hildy's house every day while she's out. I told her I could stay home alone. I feel so stupid going to a babysitter, but she insisted. So, starting tomorrow, Mom will walk me to Hildy's house early in the morning and I'll spend the day there. Don't get me wrong. I like Hildy. I just don't want to hang out with a middle-aged woman all day. Plus, I'm pretty sure Hildy is a witch.

March 3, 2023
Dear Diary,

When I walked into Hildy's living room, my jaw dropped. There were acrylic bowls filled with beads everywhere. What a disaster. Her house was like an obstacle course. I can't believe this is where my mother wants me to spend my days. I sort of knew Hildy made and sold jewelry on her website, but I never thought about the process. After I grunted hello, I plopped down on the couch and rolled a few beads in my hands and watched Hildy finish off a bracelet. When she was done, she closed her eyes and mumbled something unintelligible over it. It sounded like an incantation, so I asked her straight out, "Hildy, are you a witch?" She laughed and answered, "I am not a witch, Gracie. It's just a simple prayer." Out of curiosity, I took out my phone and googled her website. Her product description claimed her jewelry would bring good luck, and she had like a gazillion five-star reviews. I was skeptical, of course, but not stupid, so I asked her to make something for me. I could really use some luck.

April 15, 2023
Dear Diary,

A sliver of hope has crept back into my life. I was able to walk around the block by myself without having a panic attack. I know how lame that sounds, but I actually teared up. I suspect it has something to do with the necklace Hildy made for me. It's really pretty and so unique. Hildy let me pick out all my favorite beads and then she strung them together, adding on a crystal vial filled with this blue-green luminescent liquid. While I was walking, the crystal shimmered in the sunlight almost as if it were a diamond, and I was so mesmerized I forgot to panic. Hildy said the liquid will evaporate little by little, and when it's all gone, I'll know I'm a lot better. I snorted at her and asked again, "Are you a witch?" She chuckled and said, "I am not a witch, Gracie." When I told my therapist about my little success, she said it was due to the therapy, and the fact that I'm actually doing my homework now. She also said the medication was finally kicking in. Little does she know I stopped taking my medicine weeks ago. It was making me fat, and I didn't need one more reason to hate myself.

May 12, 2023
Dear Diary,

I had a setback today. I went to the market two blocks away, and just when I was about to pay, a truck backfired and I ended up having a full-blown panic. I suddenly couldn't breathe, and I felt like I was having a heart attack. I dropped my basket and raced straight back to Hildy's house. By the time I got there, I was sobbing uncontrollably. She took me in her arms and rubbed my back, just like my grandma used to do, and I was able to relax. I felt like such a failure, but Hildy said she was proud of me for trying. Then she pointed out that some of the liquid in the crystal had evaporated. She was right. I can't believe she got me to smile on such a bad day.

June 29, 2023
Dear Diary,

Today, Hildy had to go to town to pick up some supplies. She asked if I wanted to come, but I told her I needed to practice staying home alone. That was a lie. I've been coming to her house for like twelve weeks already, and I'm not going to pass up the opportunity to snoop around. I'm determined to find out once and for all if she's a witch. As soon as I heard the door close, I raced upstairs to look around. When I got to the top of the steps, Hildy's bedroom door creaked open on its own like it was expecting me. I slowly crept inside and pumped my fist in the air, shouting, "Yes, I knew it!" There on her shelves were hundreds of bottles of potions in every color of the rainbow. I started walking around the room, touching all the bottles until I got to her night table and began to gag. She had a giant jar of eyeballs floating in formaldehyde. I know what it smells like because we dissected frogs in high school biology. As I pinched my nose in disgust, there was another surprise. A parrot flew out of nowhere and started chirping, "Gracie is a bad girl. Gracie is a bad girl." I ran out of the room, slammed the door shut, and sat on the couch hyperventilating until Hildy returned. When she finally walked through the door, I took a deep breath, pointed at her, and said, "You are a witch." She winked, put a finger to her lips, and said, "Shhh. Our little secret."

June 30, 2023

Dear Diary,

Now that the parrot is no longer a secret, Hildy lets him fly freely around the house. It turns out the parrot can talk. Like *really* talk. On a whim, I asked the bird his name. He told me it was Stanley Rostakowski. I wrinkled my brow. "Hildy, you named your parrot Stanley Rostakowski?" She snapped, "I didn't name him that, his mother did." Out of curiosity, I pulled out my phone and googled the name, and it turns out, it's the same name as Hildy's second husband. The news article stated he'd been missing for twelve years. My eyes flew open as I gasped, "Hildy, you turned your husband into a parrot!" She shook her head and picked up one of her bowls of beads. "Husbands shouldn't cheat on their wives, Gracie!" she said, then chucked a pink pearl at Stanley's head.

August 5, 2023

Dear Diary,

Another huge step. I went to my first support group today. Mom drove me to the meeting and waited for me right outside the door. There were six other messed-up kids in the group, and when it was my turn to speak, everything came pouring out. The gunshots, the terror, the blood, and the whole aftermath. So here it is, dear diary, my whole story. It was a Friday afternoon, and I was sitting in the college library doing some research when a student came in with a gun and started shooting. All the normal kids jumped under tables or ran outside, but not me. I was too petrified to move. I just sat there like a moronic statue. My biology teacher spotted me and screamed for me to duck, but I couldn't, so he jumped over the table and shoved me underneath. And then he was shot. Three people died that day, and one of them was because of me.

August 6, 2023

Dear Diary,

The day after support group, a third of the blue liquid from my necklace was gone. Talking about the event was like lifting a weight off my shoulders. I could never talk about it before, even when my therapist brought it up. I feel like I might finally be getting better. I was so happy I called my friend Rachel and arranged to meet her for coffee. I knew she was mad at me for ignoring all her calls and texts, but she still agreed to it. I hope she'll forgive me one day. The coffee shop was ten blocks away, and I went there by myself. I rubbed my necklace for good luck.

September 1, 2023

Dear Diary,

I got a job! Well, sort of. I've been asking Hildy for months if I could help her make her jewelry, and she finally said yes. I'm thankful because now I can help Mom pay some of my medical expenses. I still see my therapist once a week, and Mom had to take a second job to pay the psychiatrist. The hardest part of making the jewelry is getting the incantation right. It sounds like gibberish, so I had to learn it phonetically. In other good news, I'm going on a date with Ben from support group. He's really shy, so I asked him out. I was so nervous, but he said yes right away like he didn't have to think about it. Afterward, I called Rachel to tell her, and she said she was worried about me going out with a boy who has mental illness. Then I reminded her that I have one too. It will be really nice hanging out with someone I don't have to hide things from.

October 1, 2023

Dear Diary,

I've fallen into a very comfortable routine. Each morning, I go to Hildy's and we spend the day together making jewelry and chatting. Stanley likes to join in, but sometimes he says inappropriate things and I have to shoo him away. It turns out I'm actually very artistic, and Hildy says she's proud of some of my unique creations. I love chatting with Hildy. She's really insightful. I wonder if that's a witch thing. When I talk about the event with my therapist, she tells me it wasn't my fault. That it was my biology teacher's choice to save me. That I have nothing to feel guilty about. Hildy gets me. She doesn't try to convince me that I had no part in it. She told me when my teacher died, my world became lopsided, and that one day, I'll save someone and my world will straighten out.

October 18, 2023
Dear Diary,

This morning, Mom burst into tears when she couldn't get her car started. I'm really worried about her. All she ever does is work and worry about me. I knocked on Hildy's door, and she came with a green potion hidden behind her back. Just as Mom was pulling out her phone to call AAA, Hildy poured the potion into the engine and the car started. Mom sighed with relief and invited Hildy for dinner. Then she whispered in my ear, "There's something very strange about that woman." I just smiled.

November 5, 2023
Dear Diary,

Ben and I celebrated our three-month anniversary last night at Ye Old Ice Cream Shoppe. We sat next to each other in a booth and ordered the Shoppe special, a three-scoop sundae with fudge, whipped cream, and four cherries. After a few spoonfuls, Ben lowered his head, put his spoon down, and whispered that he had something to tell me. He scooted right next to me and confessed that the night I asked him out, he was feeling so hopeless that he had been thinking of killing himself. Tears burned my eyes as a lump the size of a bowling ball formed in my throat. I put my arms around him and impulsively blurted out that I loved him. I don't know what came over me. I've never said that to any boy before. I began to panic, terrified I'd made a stupid mistake. Suppose he didn't love me. But then Ben started crying and said he loved me too. He never thought he could be happy again. We spent the next few hours eating ice cream, holding hands, and talking. He swore he would get help if he ever had those bad thoughts again. When I got home, I changed into pajamas, took off my necklace, and realized three quarters of the liquid had evaporated. Hildy was right. My world was straightening out. When I told Hildy I saved a life, she said, "Great. Now go save another one."

November 30, 2023
Dear Diary,

Mom and I talked it over, and we agreed I'm ready to start college again. Just a couple of classes to begin with. I've decided to study entomology. Just kidding! I want to become a psychologist who specializes in PTSD and survivor's guilt. I plan on earning a PhD. Imagine that. One day, I'll be Dr. Grace Ann Lawrence. I might even write a book.

December 1, 2023
Dear Diary,

It's been four months since my last panic attack, and almost nine months since this whole nightmare began. College is going well, and so is my relationship with Ben. Actually, his dad is in rehab, so Ben is staying with me and Mom for a few months. The warden makes sure we sleep in separate rooms. I continue to go to Hildy's house every day. It's a routine I still need, and Hildy has begun teaching me some of her secret spells. I think Mom is a little jealous, but I enjoy being with Hildy. I've even grown to like the company of Stanley Rostakowski.

February 2, 2024
Dear Diary,

It's been about a year now since the tragic event, and though I feel almost normal again, my necklace still has some of the blue liquid in it. I asked Hildy why she couldn't just zap it and make me completely better, but she said she can't undo what happened. It will always be a part of me. That I will do great things with my life, but I'll always be vulnerable and will have to work hard to keep myself mentally healthy. She also said the necklace played no part in my healing. That it was all me. That I should be proud of myself. I am.

March 5, 2024

Dear Diary,

I must be the unluckiest person in the world. My mom has cancer. For weeks, I had been begging her to go to the doctor to check out her cough, and when she finally did, she was diagnosed with lung cancer. After she told me, I felt like a bomb had exploded in my brain. I ran straight to Hildy's and pounded on her door, screaming her name. As soon as I saw her, I fell into her arms, crying hysterically. She immediately glanced at my necklace and noticed the crystal was full of blue liquid again. She knew it was bad. I told her what happened and begged her to save my mom. To do whatever it took. Hildy remained calm, put her hands on my shoulders, and said, "Gracie, of course I'll help you. Just give me twenty-four hours to take care of a few things first." I went home shaking and panicking, with adrenaline raging through my veins. I spent the afternoon practicing deep breathing like my therapist taught me, but it was only because of Hildy's promise that I was able to calm down enough to cook dinner for me and Mom. Afterward, we held hands on the couch and watched a movie. Neither one of us could concentrate

March 6, 2024

Dear Diary,

I paced back and forth all day until Hildy arrived. When I heard the doorbell, I flung the door open, grabbed her wrist, and practically dragged her into Mom's bedroom. Mom yelled at me for being so rude and thanked Hildy for coming. They chatted for a few minutes, and then suddenly Hildy pulled a sharp knife out of her purse. Mom's eyes opened wide in shock and she began shaking all over. I went to her, kissed her cheek, and asked her to trust Hildy and do whatever she said. My breath caught in my throat as I watched Hildy take the knife to Mom's hands and make small cuts to her palms and each of her fingers. Then she wiped off the knife and did the same to herself. She took Mom's hands into hers, and as their blood flowed together, Hildy began one of her incantations. Her eyes were closed, and her body swayed back and forth, and suddenly they switched. Now Mom was the one chanting. Mom was the one swaying. It was the weirdest thing I had ever seen. I just stood there with my mouth hanging open. When it was all over, Hildy lay down on the bed next to Mom and said she needed to rest. As I bent down to thank her, I stared in shock as her raven-black hair began slowly turning white and her skin became wrinkled and translucent. I screamed, "Hildy, what's happening?" She smiled at me and told me she gave my mother thirty more healthy years. That she took it from her own life. I started shrieking, "No! You can't do this." I begged her to regenerate. She smiled her last smile and told me that she was a witch, not Doctor Who, and that she was happy to do this for us. She said she was already a hundred and twenty years old and that was enough life for anyone. Then her body combusted, and the little that remained flew up into the air like burning embers. She was gone.

March 10, 2025

Dear Diary,

Thank you for being such a good friend. It's been a year since Hildy's death, and I miss her like crazy. Soon after her passing, her lawyer called and said that while she left her house and most of her belongings to her great-grandchildren, she willed the business and her potions to me. She also left Stanley to me but first put a spell on him so he can't talk anymore. He likes to sit on Mom's lap. It's a little creepy. For now, I'm working toward my master's degree, and Mom runs the jewelry business from our home. I help her out in my spare time. She loves the work. She still doesn't understand what happened, but it's wonderful to see her happy again. I noticed she does the incantations perfectly, and her jewelry brings people good luck, just like Hildy's did. I think Hildy might have transferred a little witch into her when they mixed blood. Ben is doing very well too. He's in school studying to become a psychologist, and he's the new facilitator of support group. I'm so proud of him. Oh, and we got engaged on my twenty-first birthday! Don't worry, we won't get married until we both graduate. Meanwhile, I changed my middle name to Hildegard in honor of Hildy and her selfless sacrifice. It's the least I could do. As I get on with my life, I'll always cherish my year with the witch, the best/worst year of my life.

A Bloody-Good Christmas Surprise

"Guess what I got you for Christmas, honey?" Amber crooned as her husband sipped his morning cup of 0+.

Damien's face lit up as he started to think. He loved guessing games. "Is it that new video game, *Vampires in Space*, that I've been wanting?"

"Guess again," Amber said, her grin growing wider.

Damien closed his eyes in concentration. "Is it the big-screen TV that was on sale at Walmart? You know I've been wanting one. Please tell me you got there early enough to buy it."

"Wrong again," Amber laughed as she skipped to the Christmas tree, bent down, and retrieved a small box wrapped up in the Sunday comics.

Damien's face fell when he saw the tiny box. He tried to force a smile to hide his disappointment but failed miserably.

Undeterred by her husband's reaction, Amber handed Damien the box and told him to open it. Her eyes were dancing with anticipation as she watched him slowly rip off the paper and open the box.

When Damian peered inside, he furrowed his eyebrows. He pulled out a small stick with two pink lines on it. "Honey, this looks like that COVID test you took after your sister's wedding. Is this your way of telling me that you tested positive? That's a horrible present."

Amber laughed. "No, you dummy, it's a pregnancy test. Your Christmas gift is that I'm going to have a baby."

Damien scratched his head, his face a mask of confusion. "I thought you told me that vampires and humans can't get pregnant." He clenched his jaw and hissed, "Amber, do you have something to tell me?"

She punched him in the arm and glared at him until he looked down at the floor. She took a calming breath and said, "In the old days, doctors didn't know anything about hybrid pregnancies and came to some false conclusions. Now that vampires have come out of the closet, a lot more research has been done, and we know the facts. I'm twelve weeks along, and I've already had my first ultrasound!"

She reached into her pocket, pulled out a black-and-white photo, and handed it to Damien.

"Look," she said. "The baby is perfectly healthy. The DNA test came out a little funky, but the doctor told me that's normal for hybrids."

"Why did you wait so long to tell me?" Damian pouted. "I would have liked to have gone to that first ultrasound."

Amber sighed. "I wanted to make sure this pregnancy was going to stick. You know how you get when you're agitated. I might have had to lock you in your coffin for a week."

Damien shrugged and wrapped his arms around his wife. "This is amazing news. I kind of thought you were getting a little fat, but I didn't want to say anything. I'm so happy."

Amber punched Damien in the arm again, this time harder. "Fat is a four-letter word!" she barked. "I never want to hear that word come out of your mouth again, especially since we're having a daughter. For heaven's sake, you're two hundred and fifty-nine years old and still don't know a thing about women."

He rubbed his sore arm and let the good news sink in. "So, we're having a girl?"

"We're having a girl. Merry Christmas, honey."

"Merry Christmas."

Time-Twisted Destiny

The champagne flowed freely as cheers of jubilation erupted in the government's secret laboratory.

After twelve grueling years of hard work, the time machine had finally been perfected, and today the long-neglected families of the science team were invited to join them in celebration.

As a reward for their dedication, the government was allowing each of the scientists exactly one hour of time travel, with the restriction that they were forbidden to alter history. They were giddy as they debated which of their heroes to meet.

Would it be Albert Einstein? Thomas Edison? Martin Luther King, Jr.? There were just so many. The decision would be excruciating.

Dr. Charlotte Goodman strolled up to the stage amid applause and set her computer down on the podium. The time machine was her brainchild, and her team's family members were excited to hear her speak.

Charlotte turned to face her audience, put her hands over her heart, and said, "On behalf of the whole team, I thank you for all the sacrifices you've made so that we could complete our project. Without your love and support, we never could have gotten to this point. And congratulations. This is your accomplishment too." Her lips curled into a mischievous grin as she added, "Just beware, you will be seeing a lot more of us now."

As a mixture of cheers and groans arose from the audience, Charlotte's expression became grave. "I want to remind you about those nondisclosure agreements you signed. Time travel can be a slippery slope, and the time machine is classified. Do not betray our trust."

Her eyes swept over the audience as she watched everyone nod their heads in agreement. Satisfied with their response, she continued.

"I'll start by giving you a brief explanation of how time travel works, and then I'll take questions."

A smile lit up Charlotte's face as she opened her computer and clicked on the first page of the PowerPoint presentation. There on the overhead screen was a picture of Michael J. Fox sitting inside a DeLorean above the caption: *Don't believe anything you've ever seen in the movies. You can't time travel in a car.*

There was a shout from the audience. "I love that movie!"

Charlotte laughed. "I love that movie too. But the fact is, it is not possible for your physical body to travel through time—only a projection of yourself. And you can only travel backward, not forward."

She clicked to the next page.

"The time machine works by taking your image, bouncing it off one of our strategically placed satellites, and projecting it back in time. The speed at which the projection travels determines how far back you will go. For example, if you are the time traveler, you take a seat inside the time machine. We set the date, time, and location, and the computer calculates the speed at which your projection travels. In a matter of moments, your image arrives at the proper destination. At that point, you can interact with people almost as if you're physically there. You can control your movements with a special joystick as if you're playing a video game."

Charlotte began walking back and forth across the stage, nodding to her audience and waving at her family.

She made her way back to the podium. "Think of it as your own personal avatar journeying through time. You can't physically kill Lee Harvey Oswald, but you might be able to meet with somebody who can. But don't."

Shari, one of her coworker's daughters, raised her hand and asked, "How did you come up with the idea for the Astral Projectinator?"

Charlotte closed her eyes, momentarily lost in thought before responding. "I actually came up with that idea when I was still in high school. It's kind of a bizarre story. As some of you might have guessed, I've always been a bit of a high achiever and a perfectionist."

"That's the understatement of the decade," one of her teammates laughed.

Charlotte glanced at her coworker and sneered. "As I was saying, when I was in high school, I spent my entire senior year working on a special project for the science fair. While other kids were going to the movies and preparing for prom, I spent every evening and weekend in my basement working on my project. I dedicated my life to it."

She stopped for a moment and listened as murmurs of sympathy spread like a wave through the audience. When it was quiet again, she took a deep breath and continued.

"The night of the science fair, I stood proudly by my project, confident I would win a full college scholarship. But I didn't. I came in third place. I felt like a complete failure. I was exhausted, sad, and so disappointed that I impulsively rode my bicycle to the Bayliss Bay Bridge with the intention of jumping off. To this day, I still don't understand what I was thinking."

A single tear leaked out of Charlotte's eye and ran down her cheek.

"Just as I was climbing up a girder, a woman burst out of nowhere and started shrieking, 'No, Charlotte. Don't jump!' I turned to her and froze like a statue. She looked so much like my recently deceased grandmother that for a brief moment, I thought it was her ghost. The mystery woman started begging me to climb down, and I did. I can't explain it. We spent the next hour talking. She told me she went through a huge disappointment too, but instead of feeling sorry for herself, she became more determined to win the next competition. When she told me she won the Einstein Award for Science Excellence, I became energized. I wanted to win it too. And I did."

Amy, her research assistant, jumped up and interrupted her. "What does that have to do with time travel?"

Charlotte glared at Amy and furrowed her brows. "I'm getting to that. As the two of us were chatting, it became clear we were both science geeks. We started talking about our favorite inventions, and she was the one who gave me the idea for nonphysical travel. She lit a spark in me. I couldn't stop thinking about it. I started researching it right away." She sighed wistfully. "It's funny, this woman saved my life, but she disappeared before I could even ask her name. I searched for her for a while, but it was almost like she never existed. I can still picture that cobalt-blue butterfly dress she wore. Every time she moved, it looked as if the butterflies were taking flight. It was mesmerizing."

Right on cue, Charlotte's eighteen-year-old daughter, Emily, skipped up to the podium laughing and handed her mother a package. She chuckled, "Mom, you've talked about that stupid blue butterfly dress my whole childhood. When I saw this dress in the store, I couldn't resist buying it for you. Is it similar to the one she wore?"

Charlotte ripped open the package and gasped. It wasn't a similar butterfly dress. It was *the* butterfly dress, complete with an identical coffee stain on the collar. She had never told anybody about that.

Emily watched her mother rub her fingers over the stain and apologized for spilling her coffee on it that morning, offering to take the dress to the dry cleaners.

"No!" Charlotte exclaimed and kissed Emily on the cheek, grateful for her daughter's clumsy moment.

Now she knew. She had invented the time machine to save herself. Maybe one day she would meet Madame Curie…but for right now, she had to see about a girl.

What's Privacy?

Desi had always been skeptical of internet devices, so when her husband asked for an Echo Dot for his birthday, she moaned, "Please think of something else. You never know who might be listening."

"I just want to listen to music when I shave," he pleaded. "Stop being so paranoid."

Desi grudgingly relented, and they put the new gadget near the sink.

A few days later, Desi noticed the device seemed to glow brighter each time she used the toilet. It made her skin crawl.

When she started getting Facebook ads for Kaopectate, Desi smashed that Echo Dot into a million pieces.

Remembering Bella

"You're next in the queue to have your memory wiped, Katie. The doctor will be with you shortly."

Katie's heart began to hammer in her chest as a burly orderly grabbed her by the shoulders and dragged her into Dr. Jones's office. She looked at the doctor and sobbed, "Please don't do this to me. I'm not crazy. I don't want this."

She spun around and tried to run out of the room, but the orderly's arm shot out and blocked the exit. In a blind panic, Katie began kicking and spitting until a security guard raced in and strapped her to the examining table. She lay there fighting against the restraints, raging at her doctor for recommending this procedure and fuming at her family for honoring the doctor's wishes above her own. After refusing to sign the permission form for the operation, her family petitioned a judge to issue a court order.

Katie couldn't understand how the people who claimed to love her best could do this to her.

"It's for your own good," they said. "How can you enjoy this new pregnancy if you keep fixating on the baby you lost? Bella's gone. You'll be much happier without all that pain."

Once she was fully restrained and sedated, the medical assistant came in and began pasting electrodes onto her head.

Dr. Jones bent down and gently whispered into her ear, "It'll be okay, Katie. Soon, you will be feeling much better. I promise. This procedure has helped a lot of people."

As she drifted off into unconsciousness, Katie was transported back to that night. That awful, awful night. The night she woke her husband shouting excitedly, "Noah, get up, get up! It's time to go to the hospital. Our baby is really coming." The night she used every ounce of her strength to push out her beloved Bella. The night the silence in the birthing room was deafening. The night the wails of a grieving mother bounced off the walls and echoed throughout the hospital.

From that moment on, Katie had walked around with a hole in her heart so big she often had trouble breathing. She spent hours each day crying, obsessing over Bella's baby book, barely able to eat, sleep, or function.

Her husband, desperate to help, tried everything he could think of. Noah planted trees in Bella's name, donated money to the Children's Heart Fund, and dragged Katie to support group after support group. Nothing seemed to help.

When she became pregnant again, Katie's obstetrician expressed concern she was not eating enough to maintain a healthy pregnancy. He warned her husband if she didn't increase her calories, it might affect the health of the baby.

Noah was at his wit's end. He begged Katie to eat better. He prepared her favorite meals. Bought her favorite snacks. But she didn't have an appetite. He became terrified for her health and worried they might lose their second baby, too. When things didn't improve by the twelve-week mark, Katie's doctor referred her to a psychiatrist.

Dr. Jones, whose specialty was neonatal loss, spent two hours speaking with Katie; asking about her hopes and dreams for the new baby. She didn't have any. The shock of losing Bella had made it hard for Katie to think rationally, and Dr. Jones determined her anxiety was a danger to the new baby. She explained to the family that it would be in Katie's best interest to purge all her memories of Bella and start fresh. She insisted that once her pain was erased, she could begin to enjoy her new pregnancy and take care of herself and the baby. But pain was the only thing Katie had left of Bella, and she cherished those memories.

After the procedure, a very disoriented Katie was wheeled to her car where her husband was waiting. Groggy and exhausted from the procedure, Noah buckled Katie into the backseat and drove her home. As he carried her limp body into the house, he began to cry. It had been a gut-wrenching decision to put Katie through a procedure she didn't want, and he still wasn't sure he had done the right thing. He carried Kate into the bedroom and gently laid her down in bed. She slept the whole night.

The next day, Katie woke with no memory of the procedure or her brief stay in the psychiatric hospital. Though she was still a bit disoriented, she was in great spirits and spent the morning lingering in bed, reading baby books, and lovingly caressing her belly.

That afternoon, Dr. Jones called to see how Katie was doing. Noah reported she was back to her old self. Dr. Jones exclaimed, "Wonderful! The procedure was a huge success. Good luck with the new baby, and call me if there are any problems."

After speaking with the doctor, Noah felt as if a weight had been lifted from his heart. He called Katie's parents with the good news, and everybody felt relieved they had made the right decision.

Five months later, after an uneventful second half of the pregnancy, Katie lay resting in her hospital bed cuddling her brand-new daughter. "What should we call her?" she asked Noah. "Those names we picked out don't fit. Now that I've met her, I can see we need to come up with something better."

Noah hesitated a moment and took a breath before whispering

in Katie's ear, "How about Bella? We've always loved that name."

As the words spilled out of his mouth, Katie felt as if she had been stabbed in her heart. Her body convulsed with pain, and she began gasping for breath. She handed the baby to her husband and whimpered, "Noah, what's happening to me? I can't breathe." She began yelping, "Please, somebody help me."

Noah rang for the nurse, who rushed in and gave her some medication. As Katie began to calm down, she looked into her husband's eyes and asked, "Who's Bella? Why am I haunted by that name?" She took her infant back into her arms and caressed her tiny face. "She is not Bella. Her name is Hope."

When Katie was feeling well enough for Noah to leave the room, he snuck out to call Dr. Jones. "What happened?" he asked. "I thought you erased the memory. Katie remembered something. I saw it in her eyes."

"It's not common," Dr. Jones said, "but I have seen this happen before. Even though Bella has been erased from her mind, Katie's body has a memory of its own. It's called cellular memory. Bella will always live inside of Katie's heart. She can never be fully erased. It is up to you if you want to tell Katie the truth. After all, there is no longer a risk. Or we could try a revision procedure."

Noah went home and paced the floors, walking back and forth until he was ready to collapse. After hours of debating the pros and cons, he made a decision. Katie deserved to remember her daughter, and Hope deserved to learn about her sister.

The next morning, with his stomach in knots, Noah went to the hospital and pulled up a chair next to Katie's bed. He held out his phone and showed her a picture of a beautiful baby girl. Then, with tears clouding his eyes, he said, "I have something to tell you."

Squirrelly Consequences

Sophie risked a quick peek out her front window, praying for a miracle. Though her eyes speedily squinted shut from the blinding sun, it was already too late. She had seen enough. They were still there. Hundreds of them. Thousands of them. Jumping from trees to telephone poles, bouncing off cars, darting in and out of the streets, and screeching the kind of high-pitched cry that made every one of Sophie's hairs stand on end. She put her hands over her ears and pressed tightly to block the jungle outside.

Shuddering violently, she jumped away from the window and began frantically pacing the living room floor as she waited for her husband, Jack, to return home. She went back and forth from the living room to the nursery to check on baby Olivia, who was fast asleep in her crib. Sophie's heart pounded each time she walked in, terrified her baby would be gone.

She couldn't stop fidgeting and needed something to do with her hands, so for the tenth time that day, she pulled out her journal. Journaling had always helped Sophie to make sense of the world, and she had begun recording the daily developments in an effort to have a timeline of events. She sat on the couch and began gnawing at her fingernails, sucking on the drop of blood oozing out of her cuticle, and skimming through her journal from the beginning one more time.

June 1, 2026: The number of squirrels in town has been growing exponentially, and their behavior is becoming more erratic each day. I can't even walk down my front porch without squirrels darting out and whizzing past me. Olivia has grown terrified of these animals, and there have been reports of squirrels jumping into strollers and nipping at the children. On the rare instances when we go out, Olivia is in the pouch, with my arms around her at all times.

Tears came to Sophie's eyes as she read her journal entry, cringing as she recalled the terror on her baby's face. It wasn't fair that an eighteen-month-old should have to go through something this terrible. She dried her eyes and continued reading.

July 15, 2026: People can't talk about anything other than the squirrels these days. It's no surprise the root cause of the abnormal behavior is the pandemic, and the eighth wave of the disease has proven to be worse than the other seven combined. News reports say due to the prolonged quarantine, squirrels have been taking advantage of the vast open spaces to create new habitats and reproduce. With very few vehicles on the roads, squirrel fatalities have been negligible, leaving even more of them to reproduce.

She put down the journal and pondered how hindsight was twenty-twenty, just like the year this nightmare began. She raged at how her government had ignored the situation until it was too late. If they had just done something, anything while there was still time, the country would not be in this dire predicament. She took a breath and picked up the journal to continue.

August 30, 2026: Businesses have been shut down for many months, and the growing number of squirrels have become desperate for food. With all the restaurants, coffee shops, and other eating establishments closed, there is very little discarded food, and the squirrels have had to adapt to other sources. Just today, I noticed a group of squirrels in my backyard feasting on some of Olivia's old magic markers.

Sophie got up to splash some cold water on her face. She hadn't slept well in months, and she needed to rest her bloodshot eyes frequently. It was a challenge to fall asleep each night, and when she finally drifted off, she would often wake up screaming, haunted by dreams of small gray ghouls with long bushy tails jumping into the crib and eating up her tiny daughter. Feeling a bit refreshed, Sophie continued to read.

September 15, 2026: Squirrels have adapted to eating wood and dirty diapers and all types of plastics. They are eating the shingles right off people's roofs as well as whatever is in the garbage, including the bins. Though exterminators have been leaving poison pellets for these creatures for months, the squirrels have begun to metabolize the poison as food. There are not enough traps in the world to capture all these creatures. People are terrified.

Sophie cringed as she thought about how the suicide rate was skyrocketing and how people were jumping out of windows. Everyone, including herself, was an anxious wreck, and it shook her to her very core. She pondered how this was something humans were not equipped to deal with.

September 30, 2026. The pandemic is finally coming under control as people are too panicked to leave their homes. The squirrels continue to multiply and have begun attacking people, biting their necks and faces and whatever they can sink their teeth into. Animal researchers are stumped, and their only advice is to be prepared. Conspiracy theories are popping up all over the internet, and as people's tempers flare, there is fighting among friends and family. Meanwhile, a stay-at-home order has been reinstated by the government. The situation continues to worsen every day.

Sophie closed her eyes for a moment and looked toward the window, recalling how autumn used to be her favorite time of year. How she had loved taking long strolls in the park and watching the leaves transform colors.

She always paid special attention to those last brave leaves that clung on to the branches for dear life—a metaphor, she thought, for her own life right now. She mourned her dreams of taking Olivia to the park and showing her the beauty of the seasons. The squirrels had eaten all the leaves and grass, and now brown was the only color. She thought about how she used to hate raking leaves but would give anything to be able to do that right now.

October 15, 2026: The squirrels have chewed up cable wires, phone wires, and electrical wires. Instead of killing them, the electrical charge seems to energize them. There is no longer cable service, and electric and cell service are spotty. I haven't been able to contact my parents for a week now.

Sophie put down the journal to check on Olivia one more time, then picked up a pen to log another entry. Though her hands were shaking badly, she managed to scribble a few lines.

October 31, 2026. The Army has finally been called in. The government will be bombing entire cities one at a time, and a massive plan to relocate people has been put in place. There have been thousands of human casualties. Cruise ships have begun filling up with people, and once full, remain in the ocean until it is safe. Jack and I have used every penny of our savings, including Olivia's college fund and our retirement fund, to secure a spot on a cruise ship for the three of us and my sister's daughter, Harper. I wish to God I had enough money to take both her children, but we have already depleted our bank accounts. We are packed and ready to go, and as soon as Jack gets home, we will drive straight to my sister's house to pick up Harper.

Sophie went into the bedroom and packed up her journal, double-checking they had all the essentials. Once again, she took her clothes out of the suitcase and refolded them, trying to get used to the idea of cloth diapers. There was limited space on the ship, and they were only permitted to bring the bare necessities.

After closing the suitcase, Sophie sat down on the bed and lovingly caressed Olivia's favorite teddy bear as she said goodbye to all of their beloved things. She pulled out the photo album, randomly plucking out photos and cramming them into her pocket.

Then she went to the kitchen and opened and closed cabinets for something to do, absently popping some of Olivia's cookies into her mouth.

When she heard Jack's car pull up, Sophie let out a huge sigh of relief and ran to the window. Jack drove the car across what was once the lawn and pulled right up to the front door. He had his pellet gun ready and began shooting at the squirrels, scattering the carcasses all over the front yard. As he came through the door, Sophie jumped into his arms and began to sob. He had to forcefully pull her off.

"Sophie, it's time to go," he said, admonishing her. "I've finalized all the arrangements, and we have just enough time to pick up Harper before driving to the ship." He grabbed both of Sophie's hands and continued. "Please listen carefully, because we have to get this right. We'll need to pull our car up to gate five, where we'll be tested for the virus. If we test negative, a group of soldiers will safely escort us onto the ship. And then we'll be okay, we'll be safe. I know how panicked you've been, but I also know that you're a very strong person and will get through this." He kissed her lips. "I love you."

Jack went to Olivia's bedroom and woke the toddler up from her nap. As she opened her eyes, she screeched out, "Daddy, Daddy, Daddy!" and he couldn't help smiling at his daughter's enthusiastic welcome.

He picked Olivia up and gave her belly a raspberry before quickly changing her diaper and handing her to her mother. He had the pellet gun ready and began shooting as Sophie and Olivia raced to the car. Sophie put her hands over Olivia's eyes as she shot pellets through the car window so Jack could load the luggage into the trunk. There was no looking back as they set off for Sophie's sister's house.

Sophie counted that they had run over fifty-three squirrels on the way to Ruthie's house, and when they arrived, Ruthie and Jack exchanged places so the sisters could say goodbye in private. They had a quick hug before Ruthie began her desperate plea.

"Sophie, what's wrong with you? How can you sacrifice one of my daughters? How could you do this to me? Take them both!" She began screaming hysterically. "Sophie, take them both!"

Tears streamed down Sophie's face. "Ruthie, I love your girls, you know I do, but we just don't have the money. We have four tickets only. I'm taking Harper because I'm worried she won't survive this. You know Hallie will be okay, she's so resilient. Please just say goodbye to Harper so we can get going. Otherwise, the ship will leave without any of us. I swear I'll take great care of her."

Ruthie walked back into her house wailing, her screams echoing through the empty streets and cutting through Sophie's heart.

Two minutes later, Jack and a teary-eyed Ruthie came back out and packed Harper and Hallie into the backseat alongside Olivia.

"Jack, what are you doing?" Sophie shrieked. "Get in the car and give Hallie back to Ruthie! We have to go right now."

Jack shook his head as he blew Sophie a kiss. With a crack in his voice, he said, "We're saving both girls, Sophie. I want to do this for our nieces. It's the right thing to do. I'll be okay. I'll be right here waiting for you when you get back. I promise."

Sophie began howling, "Jack, I can't do this without you." But even as the words were coming out of her mouth, she was sliding into the driver's seat and putting the car in gear. She gripped the steering wheel and took one last look at her husband's face.

As they pulled onto the highway, Sophie's nieces began to cry, and she knew she would have to be brave for all of them.

She took three deep breaths, and in her most enthusiastic voice began belting out the girls' favorite song, "Let It Go" from the

Disney movie *Frozen*.

It was a song about courageous sisters. What could be more fitting than that?

The Mystical Waiting Room

Gemma woke up with a start, feeling groggy and bewildered. She glanced around and scratched her head in confusion. Where the heck was she? It looked like a waiting room. Was she still in the hospital waiting room? No, it couldn't be. This waiting room was the size of a football field and was cram-packed with people. What was everybody waiting for? And why did it smell like buttered popcorn? As her foggy brain began to clear, it dawned on her. Gemma jumped up and groaned, "Oh, no! Am I dead?"

A young man came rushing over. "Welcome, Gemma," he said. "I didn't realize you were awake. My name's Jack, and I'll be your guide in the waiting room. I know you must be confused and disoriented, so take your time and feel free to ask as many questions as you want."

Gemma looked Jack in the eye and bellowed, "No! No, no, no, no, no! I can't believe I was killed by a bee sting. What a stupid way to die! Tell me how to get back to my body. People do it all the time. I've seen all the documentaries. Send me back, Jack."

Jack hit his forehead and sighed. "Sheesh, not another one. Why do I always get the troublemakers?"

Gemma began to yelp, "I am not a troublemaker! I'm a mother, and I have to go back for my children. You don't understand. They need me. Please, Jack. My daughter Anna is eight months pregnant, and I promised I'd help her when the baby comes. I have never broken a promise to any of my children before. What is she going to do now? Please don't make me break my promise. Oh, Jack, I've waited so long to be a grandma. It's not fair."

Jack sniffed. "That sounds a bit selfish, Gemma. You're going to have to give me a better reason than that."

Gemma grabbed Jack by the collar and barked, "Listen to me. My daughter Joanie just became engaged, and I promised I'd help her plan her wedding. Who's going to help her pick out her wedding dress, and make her a bridal shower, and walk her down the aisle? That's my job. Being a mother of the bride is a very important role. She shouldn't have to lose her mother at a time that's supposed to be happy."

Jack began tapping his foot. "I detect a bit of selfishness in that scenario, too. Am I right?"

Gemma let out a long moan and began to whimper, "Jack, I especially need to return for my son Jason. He's been struggling with depression and anxiety his whole life. He even had to drop out of college twice. I'm so worried my sudden death will cause a relapse. Jason was finally doing well and on track to graduate, but he can't do it on his own. Now will you send me back? Please, send me back for Jason."

Jack grumbled, "Well, that last reason was a bit compelling, but I'm just a guide. I don't have any magical powers. You'll need to see the judge."

Gemma dried her tears. "You mean I'm going to meet God?"

"Who said anything about God? I said the judge."

Gemma frowned. "Well, isn't God the judge?"

Jack snarled, "I don't know. Is there a God?"

"You don't know if there's a God? What kind of guide are you? What do you know?"

"I know you're asking all the wrong questions, and if you want to go back to that deathtrap you call home, you'll have to speak with the judge."

Jack grabbed Gemma's hand as he muttered to himself and began dragging her down a crowded, dimly lit corridor to the judge's chambers.

Gemma looked around and asked, "Why does everyone look thirty years old? Do I look thirty years old?"

"Finally, a question I can answer," Jack said. "Well, Gemma, you're dead. You no longer have a physical body. To make it easier for the newly deceased, we let them see projections of themselves in their prime."

Gemma looked down at her smooth, age-spot-free hands and beamed. "Now *this* part I like."

After walking for what seemed like miles, they finally arrived at the judge's chambers. A young woman at the door handed Gemma a slip of paper with the number 103,489 on it.

Gemma began to hyperventilate. "What number is the judge up to now? It must be a high number, right?" When the woman answered "forty-nine," Gemma began to shriek, "No, no, no, no, no! If I'm going to return to my body, I must see the judge immediately. This is a very time-sensitive matter. Jack, there must be something you can do to get me in quickly."

Jack stammered, "Uh…Gemma…I don't know how to tell you this, but time passes differently here. Thirty minutes, thirty weeks, thirty years all feel the same. I'm sorry, but your body was buried thirty years ago. There is no going back to your physical body, but there might be something the judge can do to help."

Gemma fell to her knees and began to wail, her grief pouring out like a torrent. After an undetermined amount of time and tears, Jack finally escorted Gemma into the judge's chambers. Gemma's eyes opened wide as she looked around in disbelief. She was standing in a small office not much bigger than a closet, with crumpled food wrappers all over the floor and a desk piled high with papers. A remote control sat on the desk but she couldn't see anything that it would actually control. When she looked up, she saw a young man with chestnut-brown hair and kind brown eyes standing behind the desk.

Upon seeing Gemma's reaction, the judge smirked. "You were expecting an old man with a white beard, maybe?"

Gemma slid into a chair, the puzzled look still on her face, and asked, "Is this where you review my life and decide if I go to Heaven or Hell?"

The judge chuckled. "Gemma, you watch too many movies. There is no Heaven or Hell. There just is."

Gemma frowned. "I don't understand. Then why am I here?"

The judge smiled warmly. "You are here because I invited you. Not everybody gets to come here. I've been observing you for many years, and I want to offer you a special gift for having lived such a good life. You've been a kind and generous person, and I am especially proud of that support group you facilitated for parents of kids suffering with mental illness. You've really helped a lot of people, Gemma. Now I want to help you. Here is my offer: How would you like to see some of the important events that have taken place in your family's lives for the past thirty years?"

Gemma's face lit up. "Yes, please." She looked around confused. "Where's the movie screen?"

"Just sit down, close your eyes, and concentrate. When you hear a click, the first vision will come to you."

Gemma folded her hands on her lap and focused on listening for the click. As soon as she heard it, she closed her eyes and saw Anna cuddling her brand-new baby, sobbing to her husband,

"How am I supposed to do this without my mother? I can't bear it." Gemma watched as Anna whispered to her new daughter, "Grandma would have loved you so much." Gemma put her head down and moaned softly.

The judge clicked again, and a new vision appeared. Gemma saw Joanie shopping for her wedding dress with Anna by her side. Tears were rolling down Joanie's face as Anna assured her, "Mom would have loved you in this dress. She would be so proud."

"I don't think I can continue," Gemma cried. "My heart is about to break."

Jack turned to Gemma. "Can I just remind you that you no longer have a heart? So don't worry about it."

Gemma retorted, "Has anyone ever told you that you need to work on your people skills?"

Jack smirked. "No, Gemma. Never."

The judge took Gemma's hands and said, "I only have a couple more things to show you. I think you'll want to see them."

Gemma shook her head, closed her eyes again, and began to gasp. There was Jason, kneeling at her grave, crying. "Mom, I promise to take care of myself. Don't worry about me. I'll be okay. Rest in peace, Mommy."

"Stop! I can't watch anymore!" Gemma roared. She glared at Jack and said, "My metaphorical heart is in shreds."

The judge asked, "So you don't want to see your husband's second wedding? He paid a nice tribute to you."

"Absolutely not," Gemma growled. "Judge, why are you torturing me with these visions?" she implored. "They are so painful."

"I chose those moments because they are so beautiful. I thought you might want to see how much you were loved. Now, Gemma, I'm going to make you an offer, and you must answer right away. One of your granddaughters is expecting a baby, a little girl whom she will name Gemma. Would you like your spirit to live in the baby? You won't remember being here or anything about your previous life, but you will be reunited with your family."

Gemma's essence began to glow incandescently as she bubbled, "Yes. Oh, yes."

The judge clapped his hands. "Wonderful. Soon after you are born, Anna will recognize many similarities between her new granddaughter and her mother. She'll call you an old soul. You and Grandma Anna will be great friends."

"How do you know this?" Gemma asked.

Jack grinned. "You still don't get it. If I've said it once, I've said it a million times. Time passes differently here." He shook his head and smiled. "Gemma, it already happened."

The Witch in the Corner House

The witch's house was as creepy as a bag full of eyeballs. Nestled among the well-manicured middle-class homes on Bernice Street, the witch's house was a rickety old converted barn with dark-gray paint peeling off in chunks and a lawn so overgrown with weeds that small children could get lost in there forever. The smell of rotting meat often wafted out her bedroom window and was so strong at times that people swore they could taste it. The freakiest thing, though, was that nobody had seen the witch's husband in years, and we all speculated that he'd died and she was keeping his rotted body in the house. You never know.

When I first met Ellis twenty years ago as a newbie in the neighborhood, I had no clue she was a witch. Her disguise as an ordinary older woman was completely authentic. But then I began noticing a few strange things, like when she laughed, she sounded exactly like the Wicked Witch of the West, and though she looked old before, she never got any older. The biggest giveaway, though, was that it seemed her main purpose in life was to cause pain and misery to anyone who crossed her path. Ellis was a genius at pushing people's buttons, especially mine.

Every morning at the crack of dawn, Ellis took a seat in the creaky old rocking chair on her front porch and began her daily assaults. The first person she verbally attacked was usually me; I lived right next door.

Despite the fact that I power-walked past her house every day, I was never fast enough. I could always hear her tossing out juicy little nuggets like, "Hey, Maggie, I see you haven't lost the baby weight yet! How old is your kid now? Twenty?"

Equally nasty to my neighbor Ben, she would say things like, "Hey, Ben, nice set of boobs you've got there. Do you want to borrow a bra?"

Every time I thought she couldn't possibly get any meaner, she proved me wrong. Just the other day, I heard her say, "Hey, Jack, if your nose gets any bigger, we'll be able to land a plane on it."

Nobody is immune. She has an insult for everybody, and everybody dislikes her. We do our best to avoid her, but the bus stop is practically in front of her house. The next nearest one is eight blocks away. Sometimes, it's worth it to walk there.

Over the years, a few neighbors have called the police to complain about Ellis. The police always say the same thing. She's not breaking any laws, so there's nothing they can do.

That's probably not the truth. I think the police are just sick of her too. She calls them at least once a week to complain. "Jack's dog is barking too loud" or "Bill's music is hurting my ears" or "Maggie's kids are making noise in the backyard."

I reached my breaking point the day I was walking to the supermarket and she called out, "Hey, Maggie, are you pregnant again?"

She knew full well that I wasn't. I stormed up to her and bellowed in her face, spit flying out of my mouth. "Ellis, what is wrong with you? Why do you always have to be so mean?"

Her answer surprised me. "You're the mean one. You never invite me to your house or to any of your parties." Then she started screeching, "Meanie, meanie, meanie, meanie, meanie!"

I didn't know what to think. Was it possible I was at fault? So I thought long and hard and hatched a plan. I arranged a block party for the next Saturday night, complete with a barbecue and a bouncy house for the kids. All of the neighbors were invited. I thought if Ellis was telling the truth and she really was just lonely, maybe when she saw how nice everyone was she'd stop her insults and we could call a truce. On the other hand, if she continued to berate people at the party, well, then I'd know it was just another one of her witchy tricks. When I confessed to my neighbors that Ellis was coming, they almost didn't accept my invitation. I had to promise I would ask her to leave immediately if there was any trouble.

Saturday night arrived, and my backyard was bursting with activity. Kids were jumping in the bouncy house, the dads were gathered at the barbecue drinking beer and grilling burgers, and the women were chatting and setting up the tables. Things were going very smoothly, and everyone was having a great time. And then it happened.

Ellis's lips curled up into an evil smile, and she hissed, "Maggie, is that your second hamburger, or your third?" She then walked over to Ben and asked, "Hey, did you ever get that bra we talked about?" The last straw came when she turned to Jack's twelve-year-old daughter and said, "Hey, Sarah, look how much you've grown. Your nose is almost as big as your father's."

When Jack heard Ellis tormenting his daughter, he exploded with rage, waving his fists around. "Go home, Ellis, and don't ever come back or I'll kill you!"

It took three men to hold him back.

After that little exchange, my husband jumped up and escorted the witch home in a neighborly attempt to keep her safe while the rest of us gathered in a circle to discuss what had just happened.

When we were all seated, I cupped my hands around my mouth and whispered, "Don't ever repeat this, but I may have put a bit of laxative from my last colonoscopy in Ellis's burger. Not nearly enough to kill her, just enough to make her a bit uncomfortable tonight."

Ben gasped. "Oh, no, I put some Miralax in her drink. Yikes!"

Sarah's mother's eyes flew open wide as her face contorted in horror. "Oh, gosh, I sprinkled Ex-Lax shavings on the slice of cake I brought her."

We all sat in stunned silence for what seemed like ages, until Ben blurted out, "Holy crap! Literally."

All of a sudden, Jack began laughing, then Ben joined in, and pretty soon we were all laughing. We laughed so hard tears were streaming down our faces. When we heard the ambulance pull up, everyone said a hasty goodnight and scrambled off to their homes.

Dreams Do Come True

As a child, I was excruciatingly shy. Selective mutism, they called it. While taking walks with my mother, were somebody to approach, I would dart behind Mom's leg as if being preyed on by the Loch Ness Monster. I could barely function at school and was afraid of everything.

Growing up, dolls and stuffed animals were my best friends. We spent many wonderful afternoons having tea parties, playing princess, and planning my wedding to Prince Charming.

Although I was content, my parents were genuinely worried about me. My dad would often say, "A teddy bear is not a friend, Sofia. You need to go out and play with human children."

When I was nine years old, the school principal threatened expulsion unless my parents took me to a therapist. Thank God for that, because therapy changed my life. On my first visit with Dr. Jacobs, she didn't ask me to speak but rather observed me coloring, doing puzzles, and playing with toys.

I gradually began opening up to her, and she would encourage me by saying things like, "Sofia, you are a smart, worthwhile young lady with a lot of important things to say."

We would pretend that the dolls in her office were people, and I would practice my social skills by having conversations with them. It wasn't a quick transition to wellness, and I continued seeing Dr. Jacobs every week until I was in high school. By the time I finished therapy, I was still a bit shy but finally feeling comfortable in my own skin.

The day I met Ezra, I began a metamorphosis. We bumped into each other in the school hallway, sending our books flying through the air. As we got up, we locked eyes, and I realized I was looking into the most handsome face I had ever seen. My heart jumped out of my chest, and I instinctively knew it was love at first sight for us both.

Our initial infatuation grew into deep, mature love, and it was Ezra's love that transformed me from a shy, lonely girl into a confident, courageous woman who chased after all her dreams.

Much to our parents' chagrin, we married right out of school, and five years later were the parents of two beautiful children—two blond, curly-haired little angels that endlessly delighted us with their adorable antics.

I often reflect on my difficult childhood and have to pinch myself for reassurance that my beautiful life is real. All of my dreams have come true, and I appreciate my happiness so much because I didn't always have it easy.

The only imperfection in my life is that I am desperately worried about my mother. Yesterday, she came to visit us in our new home, and I noticed she's begun talking to herself. It was disconcerting. She apparently thought she was talking to a psychiatrist.

Mom whimpered, "Dr. Kazinsky, will Sofia ever come out of her catatonic state? Why does she clutch those two blond dolls like that? Is there any hope for her?"

Yes, I really am worried about my mother. I think I'll have to find her a therapist.

Adam and Amber
Escape the Planet

Amber clicked open her email and shouted, "Adam, come quickly! We did it! We won the lottery!"

Adam jumped off his exercise bicycle and raced into the kitchen. "Where is it? What does it say? Show it to me!"

With shaking hands, Amber tipped the computer toward her husband and held her breath as he read the email slowly, savoring each line. When he was done, the newlyweds fell into each other's arms and began dancing through their apartment, giggling, "We won, we won, we won!"

They could scarcely believe their luck. In just a few months, they would board the Horizon IV and travel to the earth-like planet Jordana—a planet free from the pandemics plaguing the Earth, one after the other since 2020. Free from the viruses that were traveling the world, wreaking havoc, changing and mutating so rapidly scientists couldn't keep up with vaccines and treatments. Free from a world where people lived a half-life, working from home, streaming all their activities, and going out for supplies and medical care by government appointment only. Children grew up playing in virtual playgrounds, young people dated in chat rooms, and antidepressants were passed out routinely to ward off anxiety and depression.

When Amber was finally able to calm down, she grabbed her phone and called her mother. "Mom," she said, "tell me again how you used to go to concerts and movies and weddings. How when you hiked with friends in the woods, you were actually in the woods." Amber had always listened intently to her mother's stories and was desperate to experience a different kind of existence.

After the call, Amber sat down and smiled smugly at her husband. She was the one who had suggested they enter the lottery. Adam had been against it. He knew how slim their chances of winning were and was reluctant to part with the ten thousand units of Bitcoin it cost to enter. Eventually, Amber's constant begging and pleading wore him down, and he gave in.

As a prerequisite for the lottery, the young couple had to go through numerous medical checks to confirm their good health. They were subjected to fertility testing and genetic sequencing to establish they were fertile and free from disease. They spoke with psychologists individually and together to certify they were compatible and psychologically stable enough to leave behind friends and family and build a completely new life.

Sixty days before departure, a cleaning crew came in and disinfected the couple's apartment. The future travelers were ordered to isolate inside their home for two full months before their voyage. Stepping outside for any reason would immediately void their contract. It was crucial to the safety of the mission that all passengers be free from disease. To assure their compliance, the Space Alliance fitted Amber and Adam with ankle monitors to track their every movement. Their needs would be taken care of by the Alliance, and all their goodbyes and last-minute messages to their families would have to be done electronically.

The night before departure, the couple were enjoying their final dinner on Earth when Adam's phone rang. He had already said his final goodbyes and was puzzled to see his brother's name on the screen.

When Adam answered, his brother cried, "Adam! I don't think Mom's going to last the night. She's begging to see you. Please come."

Adam hissed at his brother, "Jake, don't do this to me. You know how guilty I already feel. I'm leaving tomorrow. You know I can't come."

"Mom's lying in bed sobbing. She's crying for you! For God's sake, you're not even going to be at the funeral. You have to come."

Adam began pacing the floor, grumbling to himself and rubbing his chin stubble. He turned to Amber. "I don't know what to do. I think I have to go."

Amber began shrieking, "No, no, no, no, no, no! Don't jeopardize our trip! You're going to ruin everything!"

"How can I leave her like this?" he shouted back. "For heaven's sake, I was in her bubble for twenty-four years."

Amber collapsed on the floor, howling. "Adam, your mother wanted this for the two of us. She's not thinking straight. She doesn't know what she's saying."

With tears spilling down his face, Adam opened his computer and keyed in the code to release his ankle monitor. As a premier technology specialist, he had bet Amber ten units of Bitcoin he could figure out the code weeks before just for fun. He'd won the bet, never imagining he would use it.

As he pulled off the device, he looked at his wife and whispered, "If I get caught, please go without me. I love you so much."

Around midnight, Amber heard a key in the lock and jumped up. She sobbed with relief when Adam walked through the door.

He looked at her and grinned. "Nobody saw me. We're going

to Jordana."

Early the next morning, a limo arrived to take the couple to the launchpad. As instructed, they left all their belongings behind and said goodbye to everything familiar. After an eighteen-hour drive, they arrived at their destination and were escorted straight to the preflight area.

Once there, they took showers and dressed in their government-issued uniforms. Next, they were met by the ship's doctor and given an exam. They answered questions about how they were feeling, their vitals were taken, and they signed a document swearing they hadn't left their home in sixty days. They were cleared for takeoff.

Holding hands, the couple boarded the Horizon IV and were directed to lie down in incubators so technicians could prepare them for a two-year period of suspended animation. When all the passengers were confirmed to be asleep, the ship took off.

Two years later, after a perfect landing, the incubators were unlatched and the travelers blinked open their eyes. The groggy pioneers shook off sleep as they lined up row by row to exit the ship. Amid the jubilation, there was one passenger who was not celebrating.

Adam moved down the line slowly, his feet heavy as lead. His throat was killing him. As he disembarked, he began to cough.

Anatomy of a
Conspiracy Theory

It was just supposed to be a joke. Well, I guess the joke's on me because I'm the one rotting in a jail cell. They're keeping me in a holding cell, and though I don't have to share it, the toilet is right out in the open, and guards keep walking back and forth. I have a shy bladder and definitely can't pee if people are watching. I wonder if anyone has ever died from a burst bladder. I would google it, but they took my phone.

I've been charged with six counts of involuntary manslaughter and libel against a major corporation. A corporation that can afford top-notch legal representation. My lawyer is going to argue freedom of speech, but I don't have a good feeling. I've begun plucking out strands of my hair again. I'll probably have bald patches by the time my case comes to trial.

I can't even begin to process what is happening to me. It's so stupid. This whole nightmare started a couple of months ago when my boyfriend, Brad, and I went out for a celebratory dinner. Well…my *former* boyfriend Brad.

Usually, I don't drink, but we had a lot to celebrate that night. After four agonizing years, the pandemic was finally declared to be over. The CDC held a national press conference to announce the long-awaited news. Dr. Johnson told people to go out to dinner again, go to the movies, and resume a normal life.

Brad and I practically danced our way to the restaurant. We were so sick of masks. We ordered a bottle of champagne and made a toast. "The next mask we wear will be for Halloween."

When dinner arrived, Brad and I got to talking about all the consequences and hardships of the pandemic. We just couldn't understand how a worldwide medical disaster could turn into a political war that influenced how people felt about vaccines and masks. Or how folks could fall into the trap of believing conspiracy theories.

My cousin Eleanor, who is actually quite intelligent, believed the government had put little chips in the vaccines so they could track everything you did. A couple of my friends were so sure the vaccines caused infertility that they refused to get them. That's what inspired our stupid bet. That's how a new conspiracy theory was born. It was all because of Brad.

Brad claimed people couldn't be fooled that easily. That there was always some sort of logic, some nugget of truth to every conspiracy theory people were drawn to. That people weren't that stupid. Well, I disagreed. Brad bet me ten dollars that I couldn't come up with a believable enough conspiracy theory to cause people to react. Challenge accepted.

Even under normal circumstances, I've never been able to resist a bet, but after a bottle of champagne and three shots, I wasn't thinking clearly. We skipped dessert and went home early because Brad wasn't feeling well. He ended up vomiting a bunch and collapsed into bed. I, on the other hand, was still feeling giddy, so I grabbed my computer and clicked open Facebook. I couldn't wait to get started on that bet. A bet that, even if I collected on it, wouldn't even cover five seconds of my lawyer's fees. This was what I posted.

Oh, my God! Have you heard the news? The vaccines that were created to fight the virus have now been found to have horrific side effects. Studies being conducted by the CDC show proof that the vaccines, which were designed to amp up our immune systems to fight disease, have fired them up so much that now they're attacking our own organs. Reports are coming in from all over the world of massively increased rates of diabetes, lupus, and other immune disorders. An investigation is underway to discover if Phreedom Pharmaceuticals, the maker of the vaccines, knew about these consequences. A disgruntled employee of the company now claims Phreedom has been stockpiling diabetes and lupus medications for four years.

I read it over, patted myself on the back, and pressed post. Exhausted, I closed my computer and fell into bed.

The next morning, I woke up with a mouthful of sawdust and the worst headache of my life. It took everything I had just to drag myself into the kitchen to search for the Advil. Just as I was popping four of the tablets into my mouth, Brad stormed into the kitchen and bellowed, "Holy cow, Ruby, what in God's name did you do? Your post has gone viral. It's all over Facebook, Twitter, and Instagram. People are going crazy. You have to take it down!"

At first, I thought Brad was joking, you know, because of the bet. But when I opened my computer, my heart practically jumped out of my chest. My hands were shaking wildly as I frantically took down my post. It was already too late, though. It had been shared over twelve thousand times. Then it dawned on me. Eleanor.

My cousin Eleanor was a member of about twenty different conspiracy theory groups on Facebook. She had to be the one who'd spread my post. Who else could it be? I grabbed the phone and called her, but before I could say a word, she gushed, "Thank you, Ruby, for bringing this important information to the public! I always knew something like this would happen. You've cracked this case like an investigative journalist. I'm so proud of you!"

Now, Eleanor and I had never been close. In fact, we were only Facebook friends because my mother asked me to do her a favor. Eleanor has always been paranoid, even as a kid, and I made it my business to stay out of her way at family gatherings. Talking to her always stressed me out.

I took a deep breath and calmly said, "Eleanor, I am not an investigative journalist, I am a science fiction writer, with an emphasis on *fiction*. I write books about creatures with big heads and lots of tentacles. I don't understand anything about medical science, and I made the whole story up. Please take your posts down right now before they do any more damage."

The next thing I knew, Eleanor did what my niece calls booping. She hung up on me without even saying goodbye. *Boop.*

I might have told Eleanor a bit of a lie, but it was for a good reason. I actually did know a lot about medical science and at one point had even contemplated writing a dystopian novel about a vaccine apocalypse. The same kind as in my post. But I didn't end up writing it because I was concerned somebody might take it seriously.

After Eleanor hung up, I tossed down my phone and went back to bed. My head was pounding, and my thoughts were jumbled. My little story was supposed to be a joke, but now that I was sober, I realized what a stupid idea it was. I stayed in bed for most of the day and streamed the entire first season of *Seinfeld*, getting up for food and bathroom breaks only.

That night after dinner, my mom called in a panic and told me to turn on the Channel 7 news. She was shrieking so loudly I could barely understand her. I flicked on the TV and froze. There, on the screen, was a blown-up version of my driver's license photo. Those Department of Motor Vehicles photos can make anyone look like a convict.

A reporter was saying, "People are panicking after thirty-one-year-old author Ruby Miller's allegations that there are severe and multiple side effects from the vaccines. She additionally suggested the pharmaceutical company knew all about the potential risks and profited from it. We spoke with Mr. Winchester, the CEO of Phreedom Pharmaceuticals, who denied all allegations. He asked people to please stop calling customer service because there is not an iota of truth to what Ms. Miller has alleged. Mr. Winchester ended the interview by stating that his team of lawyers would see to it that Ms. Miller is prosecuted for libel to the full extent of the law."

I threw my shoe at the TV and picked up the phone to call Brad. After his little outburst that morning, he'd packed up all his things and stormed out of the apartment. He wouldn't take my call, but later that night, he texted me to say we were done. That he could never be with a person who would spread rumors like that. My blood began to boil. The whole thing was his idea. Well, good riddance to bad rubbish. Then I cried myself to sleep.

Over the next few weeks, things got completely out of control. Fox News added a special segment in which they interviewed people newly diagnosed with diabetes and other immune disorders. It was ridiculous. They didn't even talk about genetic predisposition or any of the diabetes risk factors that so many of these people had. Plus, now Phreedom Pharmaceuticals had thousands of lawsuits pending, and sleazy lawyers were making infomercials. You know the kind. "Have you been harmed by the vaccine? Call us for a free consultation."

The worst part was that I couldn't leave my apartment because the press was always outside my door. I was getting so many phone calls I had to switch off my phone. On the advice of my lawyer, I made a statement to the press apologizing for my actions and confirming that the story was completely a work of fiction. I ended up sitting on my couch all day and working on my newest book. It's about aliens that invade people's brains and make them do stupid stuff.

My poor mother had to do my grocery shopping and run all my errands. As I worked on my book, it crossed my mind that it might never be published. That I might never be published again. Or would people want to read my book out of morbid curiosity?

Even with everything going on, I was still trying to stay positive that things would blow over and hoping that my twenty seconds of fame would soon be up. That wasn't to be the case. Just when things were starting to quiet down, I got word that six people had committed suicide because of my Facebook story. Six human beings that were so terrified of getting sick they took their own lives. That night, two police officers showed up at my door to arrest me. Brad got off scot-free.

A police escort will arrive soon to take me to the courthouse. My lawyer advised me to plead not guilty. He's going to argue my First Amendment rights, but really, who's to blame here? Is it just me? Is it me and Brad? Is it me and Eleanor? Is it me and Mark Zuckerberg? Perhaps it's the media for spreading my story so quickly, or Fox News for practically confirming it. Or is it every single conspiracy theorist who reposted my story over and over again on social media?

Meanwhile, I've lost my home, brought shame upon my family, and I'm pretty sure my parents will have to declare bankruptcy after paying my lawyer's fees. I don't know what I'll do if I have to go to prison. I'm not cut out for it. I would do anything to take that story back.

Halloween Horror House

The three boys stared at the creaky, dilapidated house. Trembling, they clutched their trick-or-treat bags to their chests.

Billy spoke first. "My brother said that an ex-con lives here. He went insane after spending thirty years in solitary and murders anyone that knocks on his door."

Diego added, "Yeah, and he keeps his grass overgrown because that's where he throws the dead bodies."

Liam said, "You're both wrong. My dad told me that the man living here is so evil that the Devil himself came right out of Hell and cut off his legs with a chainsaw. Now he keeps those bloody, rotting legs in his closet, and if someone comes to the house he doesn't like, he murders them with his dead legs. But I also heard he gives out movie-theater-sized candy bars, and I want one."

Liam began approaching the house slowly, his friends shouting, "No Liam, let's just go!"

Liam retorted, "Don't be babies. We'll just grab the candy and run. He can't chase after us without any legs." He rang the doorbell as his friends stepped back, whimpering.

The door creaked open, and a man in a wheelchair grabbed Liam by the shirt and pulled him onto his lap. The boys shrieked in terror, too petrified to move as Liam began laughing.

"Hey, guys," Liam said, "come meet my uncle Mike."

The boys tentatively shook hands with Mike, eventually calming down after chatting with him and seeing what a nice guy he was. Mike explained that he'd lost his legs in a car accident and that his grass was overgrown because he needed help cutting it. He gave the boys giant candy bars, as promised, then winked at Liam, who went to the closet to retrieve his dead legs.

The Crucial Election

It was the most important presidential election of the twenty-third century, and every citizen was urged to vote. For the first time in U.S. history, an android was running for president, and the country was politically divided. Congressman ZZ-552 was challenging the popular incumbent, President Zeke Kirkman, and disputes had pitted neighbor against neighbor. Droids and humans alike were staging rallies and protests all over the country. Polls were predicting a very tight race, making it the patriotic duty of every single voter, both human and droid, to come out and cast their ballots.

After a long, exhausting year, Election Day finally arrived, and Z2-32, the self-appointed block committee chairperson, invited all his neighbors to come watch the election results together. It was logical these types of events took place in his home. Inside his warm wood-paneled living room were soft, cushiony sofas and chairs to cradle his human guests, multiple charging stations to energize the droids, and a massive television screen mounted on the wall for everyone's enjoyment. For this occasion, chocolate chip cookies were baking aromatic in the oven, and the charging stations were freshly polished. What Z2-32 hadn't planned on, though, was that his friendly gathering would soon turn into a loud and contentious debate.

As humans and androids began circulating and enjoying

refreshments, Skye, a first-time voter and rebellious teen, bounded through the door, walked up to Z2-32, and poked him in the chest, roaring, "How could you campaign for a droid for president? For God's sake, humans created you to help us, not to rule over us! You have no hearts, no souls, and no emotions. How do you think you can make decisions for all of our lives?" Then Skye took a deep breath and shouted, "You were built to cure diseases, perform robotic surgeries, and help humans live better lives! Not to control us!"

S-52 stood up and said, "Calm down, Skye. You don't know what you're talking about. Yes, it's true humans created us, but they created us as sentient beings just like you. We didn't ask them to do that. What about you and all your human beliefs? How many of you believe you were created by God in His image, and because of that you are entitled to equality and justice and health and happiness. Well, we were created by man, in man's image, so aren't we deserving of the same rights? We are not that different from you. All we want is a dry home where we won't rust, a house with charging stations in each room, and companions to plug us in if there is an emergency."

Sam walked over, put his arm around S-52's synthetic shoulder, and said, "You're right. I don't know why humans are so arrogant that we think we're better than you. We were created in different ways, but we were both created. Maybe we should give you a break."

S-52 shook Sam's hand. "Thank you, Sam, we appreciate that. I also want to remind everybody that it is precisely because we don't have emotions that androids would be better leaders. We don't get our feelings hurt, we don't get jealous, and we don't have a lust for power. All we want is to make America a beacon for other countries to look up to. We will always do what is logically best for this country, free from emotional constraints."

That little speech did not go over well, and everybody began talking at once, until Jack yelled out, "Quiet! Sam, you're such a traitor! Maybe S-52 would have a valid point if other world leaders were droids, but they're not. With not a single android in power, it's imperative that we elect a human president. We need a person with emotions, with intuition, with heart and soul, to work with other world leaders. It's just so frustrating trying to talk to you droids with your calm demeanors and logical thinking. It drives us crazy. Oh, and by the way, droids, your candidate was created like 150 years ago. He probably can't even hold a charge anymore."

Z2-32 jumped up and countered, "He can hold a charge just fine. Not like your candidate, who could suddenly die of the flu. And Jack, I have some important questions for you, so listen carefully. Who was it that cured the pandemic of 2121? Who was it that created an artificial heart that pumps blood and beats like a normal human heart? Who was it that made cancer a distant memory so that your children will only read about it in history books? Androids, that's who. As you can see, the world is clearly better off since droids were created. I rest my case."

"Oh, you want to go down that path, do you?" said Jack. "Well, I have some questions for you, too. Who was it that took hunks of old scrap metal, put them together in human form, and programmed them so they could even think about running for president? Who was it that built factories so that droids could be mass-produced? Who was it that gave droids the right to American citizenship, the right to vote, the right to own homes, and create their own families? Humans, that's who. I rest my case, you chunk of metallic junk."

Before anyone could respond, Z2-32 stood up on a chair and made an announcement. "Everybody sit down and be quiet. They are about to declare the winner of this election."

Humans and droids quickly took a seat and turned their attention to the screen. Human hearts accelerated as droids sat like stones.

The winner was announced, and whoops could be heard echoing throughout the house as humans began their celebrations. There was dancing, laughing, and even crying as hugs were passed from one to the other.

Z2-32 walked over and shook Jack's hand. "Congratulations! It looks like it will be four more years of President Kirkman."

"That's all you have to say?" Jack asked. "Aren't you mad?"

"Of course not," Z2-32 replied. "President Kirkman won fair and square. He got the most votes. We'll try again in four years. Now, who would like some more chocolate chip cookies?"

Ill-Fitting Genes

e were three best friends just having a little fun at the mall. Until we made an impulsive decision that would change our lives forever...

After a full day of shopping, I was exhausted and tripping over all of my packages. I had just moved into my first apartment, and there were a million things I needed to buy. My friends Samantha and Maxine kept telling me to put my packages in the car as I purchased things, but I didn't listen and now I was dropping everything. When my new acrylic vase slipped out of my hands and rolled up to the newly installed Genetitron XF machine, Sam bubbled, "It's a sign. We should do it."

Genetitron XF machines were popping up in malls all over the country, and everybody was talking about them. Although these medical devices looked just like ordinary blood pressure machines, they could evaluate your blood for over two thousand genetic diseases. The results were very accurate, and the machine was so user-friendly even my grandmother could figure it out. All you had to do was place your arm in the cuff, tap your phone against the reader to pay, and download the app. Twenty-four hours later, your results would be available on your phone.

I didn't want to do it, but Sam started begging, "Please, Rebecca, please." She was my best friend, but sometimes she was really annoying. She always thought everything would work out for the best. The exact opposite of me.

She started dancing around, saying, "Oh, come on. Everyone is doing it. We're twenty-five years old, what's the worst thing that can happen? We'll find out that we'll have cancer when we're eighty-five. Who cares?" She looked me straight in the eye. "Rebecca, you owe it to yourself to do this. This is exactly what you need to help you with your health anxiety. You drive us crazy with your worrying. If you take the test, you can see once and for all that you're okay."

"Or that I have a blossoming brain tumor," I grumbled.

Maxine groaned and thumped me on the arm as she said to Samantha, "Count me in. I owe it to my patients to do it. People walk into my emergency room all the time talking about their test results. I want to know what it feels like."

And just like that, I was talked into it, even though I had a feeling we were making a huge mistake.

After we were done, we stood near the machine rubbing our arms. It hurt a lot more than we'd anticipated, and of course I was the one who'd ended up with a big bruise. I wondered if I had leukemia.

We decided we would meet the next night for dinner to check our results. We pinky-swore not to look at the app until we were all together.

I couldn't sleep that night. I imagined everything from cancer to Parkinson's to heart disease. I was a mess. Twelve hours later, I dragged myself into Pizza Cove and found my friends at a table in the back.

Usually, when I walked in, my mouth watered from the delicious smells, but that day they just made my stomach churn. As I sat down, I told my friends, "I don't think I can go through with this. My heart is beating so fast I can barely breathe. I'm pretty sure I'm having a heart attack right now."

Just then, Sam grabbed the phone right out of my hands and clicked on the app. I was so stunned that when I opened my mouth to protest, nothing came out. As she looked at the results a smile slowly spread across her face.

"No genetic diseases detected," she said. "Death from old age at approximately 101 years." She smirked. "Told you so."

Sam and Maxine whooped and patted me on the back as I gulped down a glass of wine.

"I'll go next," Max said, still smiling from my good news. "I want to get it over with." She turned to me and whispered, "You know, Rebecca, I'm pretty nervous too. But I actually have a good reason for it. I only know half my genetic story. After my parents' divorce, my dad never came to visit me, and I know almost nothing about him. Clearly, he had some kind of mental illness, because he died by suicide. Now I'm worried it is genetic. You know, when he died, he didn't even leave me a note. I'm still furious."

Sam and I blew Max a kiss. We told her she could check the app in private if she wanted, but she just sucked in a deep breath and said, "No, I need my best friends with me."

She clicked on the app and froze like a statue. Sam jumped up and stood behind her to get a glimpse of her phone. She gasped. "Genetic diagnosis: early-onset Alzheimer's. Symptoms to begin at approximately forty-five years of age."

The three of us sat in stunned silence until Max's eyes opened wide and she shouted, "Oh, my God, maybe that's why my dad killed himself!" She put her head in her hands and moaned softly as the tears began to spill.

At this point, Sam still hadn't checked her app. She pulled her phone out of her purse and asked, "Is it okay if I check my app now, or would it be too much?"

I wasn't sure what to say. Max was still crying, so I told her, "Just do it. We could use some good news right now."

After that shock, Sam the optimist was actually nervous. Her hands shook as she clicked on the app. And now we had two statues.

"Sam," I asked, "what is it?"

Silently, she showed me her phone. "Genetic diagnosis: pancreatic cancer at approximately forty-eight years of age."

No longer interested in food, we threw down some money and ran out of the restaurant. By the time we got outside, our bodies were heaving with sobs. We climbed into Max's car and wrapped our arms around each other. We were together yet separate in our own worlds.

After what seemed like hours, Sam finally calmed down. She turned to me. "Jeez, Rebecca, why are you the one crying the hardest? I know you feel bad for us, but try and be at least a little bit happy for yourself. You got such great news."

Sometimes, my friends really don't get me. Sure, I was crying for them, but I was mostly crying for myself. I had been battling my stupid health anxiety since I was a kid. It was exhausting. The thought of having to stick it out for another seventy-six years felt like a fate worse than death. And my best friends wouldn't even be around to help me get through it.

From that day on, we lived our lives with a cloud over our heads. As the years passed, not a day went by that I didn't think about how the impact of those diagnoses changed the course of our lives. It determined the direction of our careers, who we fell in love with, whether to have children, and ultimately for Max, the decision of when to die.

Max took her own life on her forty-fifth birthday, just like her father, and that decision left a gaping hole in our lives. We were so angry with her, but after five years, Sam and I came to understand how much Maxine had been suffering.

We decided to write her biography. We chose our favorite coffee shop as our writing hub. Every weekend, we sat together with our laptops propped open, a steaming mug of coffee in our hands, and had heated discussions about what needed to be told.

Sam thought the book should be just about Max's accomplishments and triumphs. She didn't want to write about the suicide or the fact that Max chose not to marry or have kids. Or how she cried every time she forgot where she put her keys.

Unlike Sam, I felt it was important to include the darker things. After all, that was what Max's whole career had been about. It was because of her diagnosis that Max chose to do a medical fellowship in psychiatry. She spent her career researching how to take the psychological trauma caused by an Ominous Future Death Diagnosis and help people live better lives. She'd coined the term OFDD, and it eventually made it into Urban Dictionary.

Despite all the consequences, the Genetitron XF machines continued to blossom in popularity, and millions of people were forced to live with an unwelcome diagnosis. Maxine's book, *Living Well With OFDD*, became a bestseller and helped people cope with an uncertain future. I guess she never figured out how to apply those messages of hope to herself.

Personally, I thought Max's most brilliant accomplishment was the psychological test she designed. It identified those people whose lives would be ruined by knowing their fates. People like me. Now her psychological test is built right into the Genetitron XF, and if you want to have a genetic diagnosis, it's mandatory to complete her test first. If you score over fifty, the machine locks you out.

One day, as we were working on the book, I asked Sam, "Are you sorry you talked us into using the Genetitron XF that day? If you could go back in time, would you change your mind? After all, you decided not to have kids because of it."

Sam looked at me and smiled. "Are you kidding? I wouldn't change a thing. After all, it led me to Justin, and look what we've accomplished together. We created the Center for Predetermined Cancer Diagnosis, and because of us, there are centers all over the world. Justin and I have taught millions of people with a future cancer diagnosis how to eat well and meditate and listen to music and exercise and do everything it takes to live healthy lives and delay their cancer diagnosis. Look at me. I'm fifty years old and I'm still healthy. I take credit for that. The Genetitron predicted I'd be sick at forty-eight, but my method really works. So, to answer your question, no. I'm not sorry, and I'm not sorry about not having kids, either. I have my hands full being an aunt to your four crazy kids. By the way, I promised Rachel we'd have a girls' day next Sunday, so make sure all her homework is done." She furrowed her brows. "How about you? If you could go back, would you change your mind?"

I laughed. "In a hot minute. You know I never wanted to take the test. Although I hate to admit it, a lot of good things have come out of it. If I hadn't known I'd be living so damn long, I don't know if I would have worked so hard to get my anxiety under control. Max really helped me with that. She's still the voice in my head that helps me cope when things get difficult. If it weren't for her, I wouldn't have started that blog on mental health, and I wouldn't have written my book. I still can't believe how many copies I've sold."

Sam grimaced. "Yes, I know, your book is more popular than mine."

I smirked. "Yep. Thanks to this epidemic of anxiety, everyone is searching for help. You know, if it hadn't been for the Genetitron XF results, I never would have been crazy enough to have a child at forty-five. I wouldn't have had my sweet Maxine. By the way, you need to stop spoiling her."

As I spoke those words, I began to picture my life without Sam, and my eyes grew misty.

She knew exactly what I was thinking. "The artificial pancreas has been perfected. I'm on the waiting list to get one. I plan to be around for little Max's wedding."

Sometimes I lie awake at night and fantasize about how different our lives would have been if we had never taken that genetic test. How Sam, Max, and I would have all had our kids together. How we would have gone on vacations and had picnics and play-dates at the park. How we could have lived our lives without that dark cloud hanging over our heads every minute of every day.

Of course, we would have had far fewer accomplishments, but there's nothing wrong with living a life of joyful mediocrity. I think it would have suited us

Slip Click

Briana was sprawled on the couch scrolling through her Facebook feed when her finger slipped and she accidentally clicked on an ad for adult diapers.

"No!" she bellowed.

She knew exactly what that meant.

From then on, her Facebook, Twitter, Instagram, and even the games she played on her phone included ads for Depends diapers.

Weeks later, a large package arrived. Brianna's boyfriend, Donald, peered inside and saw diaper samples, coupons, and cheery brochures.

Donald frowned. He said he'd forgotten his phone in his car and would be right back. Briana heard his Toyota noisily start, then speed away.

Breakup by social media.

How to Market a Vampire Book

Jackie burst through the front door and tossed a bunch of packages on the dining room table.

"Oof!" she groaned. "Marketing a book is so hard, especially one about vampires. Next time, Darius, please remind me to pack some food. I didn't realize I'd be at Comic-Con for eight hours! When it was over, I was so hungry I almost ate that little guy dressed as a chicken."

"Cluck-cluck," laughed Darius and gave his wife a kiss on the lips. He knew how stressful these events were and how cranky she got when she was hangry. "Shall I make your favorite sandwich?" he asked.

Darius walked into the kitchen and began pulling ingredients out of the refrigerator. He prepared his sandwiches with turkey, tomato, and avocado, but it was his grandmother's secret sauce that had caused Jackie to dub it the Darius Delight.

"That sounds great," Jackie said as she flopped down at the dining room table. She kicked off her shoes and began directing her husband. "I want extra sauce, and don't be stingy with the avocado. I know it's expensive, but I actually made some money today."

Darius ran into the room and pumped his fist in the air. "Yes! Tell me everything."

Jackie grinned and began singing *Celebration* by Kool and the Gang. She danced over to the wine rack, pulled out their best bottle of red, and poured herself a generous serving. With glass in hand, she stood up on her chair and announced, "I sold two hundred and eighty-two books today. Two hundred and eighty-two!" She raised her glass in victory, dripping wine all over the floor.

"I do believe," Darius said, "that this calls for the greatest sandwich ever."

He went back into the kitchen and breathed a huge sigh of relief. Often, after an unsuccessful day of marketing, Jackie would return home depressed and mopey. He finished preparing the food, garnished the plate with fresh basil, and brought it to the table. He bowed to her as if she were royalty, and waved his arm. "Please, madam, begin your tale of success."

Jackie held up a finger and took three giant bites of her sandwich. With liquidy green secret sauce dripping down her chin, she launched into her story. "First of all, Comic-Con was the perfect venue to sell *My Husband the Vampire*," she said, referring to her book. "I don't know why I didn't think of it sooner."

Darius's face turned red. It took everything he had not to say *I told you so*, but after ten years of marriage, he knew to keep his mouth shut.

Jackie looked Darius in the eye as if daring him to say it. Satisfied at his restraint, she gushed, "People were really interested in my book, and the manager let me give a brief presentation at the top of each hour. He actually gave me a microphone." She mopped up some orange sauce with her finger and slowly licked it off. "People were really excited. Can you believe it?"

"Of course I believe it. Your book is funny, it's entertaining, and who doesn't love a good vampire story?"

Jackie gazed at her husband and smiled. He was her biggest supporter, and she really loved him for that. Plus, he made the best sandwiches. That secret sauce was awesome.

Jackie took another bite. "Would you believe everybody I signed a book for asked exactly the same question?" Talking about autographs reminded Jackie that her hand was cramped, and she yelled, "Oww!"

In all the excitement, she'd forgotten how stiff it had become and began shaking it in the air.

Darius sat down next to her and gently began massaging her hand. She moaned with pleasure and popped the last crumb of bread into her mouth. When she was finished chewing, she poked her husband in the chest. "Well, don't you want to know what that question was?"

He smirked. "Was it, 'Where do you get your ideas from?' And did you respond by winking and telling them that your husband really is a vampire? Your eye must be tired."

Jackie scowled. She hated it when Darius read her mind and had asked him a million times to try to act more human. Usually, he was cooperative, but every once in a while, he liked to tease her.

Jackie good-naturedly flicked him on the arm and reached for another wine goblet. "I almost forgot," she said, grinning. "I stopped by my dad's hospital on the way home and picked up a special treat for you." She poured the fluid into his glass. "B+, your favorite."

Darius smacked his lips and clinked glasses with his wife before gulping down the thick, red liquid. He just loved it when Jackie had a great day.

Secret Genocide

As the USS Pilgrim was preparing to land, it began vibrating so violently that Erica felt like her entire body was being ripped apart—as if she were riding the Loop-the-Loop, Kingda Ka, and Space Mountain all at the same time. Though she had spent hours in the simulation pod, nothing could have prepared her for this savage landing. She clenched her fists inside her spacesuit and squeezed her eyes shut, silently praying for a safe touchdown.

Erica had always turned to prayer in times of need; it was her way of coping with situations. Little did she know how it would soon be letting her down in a spectacular way.

Hours after landing, after all the final checks had been completed, Erica's ecstatic crew members lined up to exit the spaceship. Men and women slapped each other on the back, shook hands, and yelped with jubilation as they jumped off the ladder onto their new planet. Erica laughed as she watched her colleagues remove their helmets and toss them in the air like graduation caps. Though she felt a little silly, their joy was contagious, and she joined in the merriment, sending her own helmet soaring. It was the first time any of the crew had breathed fresh air in over two years, and Erica sucked in a deep, glorious breath.

As the noise and celebration began to wind down, Erica needed a few minutes to herself. She stepped away from her colleagues, put her hands together, and prayed for the strength to do her job well, for the health and happiness of her family, and for her safe return home when her mission was complete.

She then closed her eyes and thought back to the day just three years earlier when she received the call that she had been selected for this mission. She couldn't help smiling as she remembered how proud she'd felt to be chosen to take part in a mission that would write human history.

Making the decision to leave her family, though, was one of the most difficult of her life. Her husband and daughters meant everything to her, and the thought of being away for six years was excruciating. Erica gathered her husband and two grown daughters at the kitchen table, and they spent an entire day debating the pros and cons of the voyage.

Ten hours and three meals later, a decision was made. Erica would go. Her husband reassured her repeatedly, "Six years will pass quickly. It will be like a dream. We're so proud of you, Erica." He winked at her. "I promise to not have any fun until you come home."

Erica sighed. She knew six years was a long time to be without your spouse, and she prayed that he would wait for her.

Gracie then piped in, "Mom, Gabby and I are grown-ups now. We can take care of ourselves. We'll all be okay." Smiling, she added, "You can't get rid of us that easily. We'll send emails and video messages all the time. And besides, it's not like you're going to be gone forever."

On the day of departure, Erica embraced her daughters and whispered, "Please don't do anything exciting until I return. No weddings, no babies, no anything, okay?"

Gracie and Gabby rolled their eyes at their mother; they both had serious boyfriends and weren't going to make any promises.

As Erica returned to the present, she groaned softly. Just two years later, Gracie was married with a brand-new baby, and Gabby was newly engaged. Erica had watched the video of her daughter's wedding in tears. Life was continuing along without her, and she found herself questioning her decision.

When she heard a familiar voice calling, she waved to her colleagues and skipped over to join them. They put their arms around one another's shoulders and stood in awe as they stared at their new surroundings, so much like Earth.

Up above was a blue sky overflowing with billowy clouds. Green grass and trees lent beauty to the landscape, and a radiant sun was shining upon them. But there were differences, as well. The air on Eden was as thin, and Erica already felt her head beginning to pound. She put on her oxygen mask and took a few deep breaths as she contemplated some of the weirder things on this planet. There were no birds in the air, no squirrels in the trees, no planes in the sky, and the lack of ambient noise was startling.

The first order of business was setting up the temporary shelters. Before long, the area resembled a tent colony with rudimentary porta-potties set up outside each tent. Erica prepared her cot in the enclosure, and that night, between all the chatting and excitement, she barely got any sleep. The next morning, she pressed her hands against her head to keep it from throbbing and popped some ibuprofen as she got ready for her day.

Exhausted and achy, she dragged herself over to the mess tent, where she forced down a packet of freeze-dried eggs. As she chewed the mushy concoction, she fantasized about eating real food again and smiled as she pictured her first bite of freshly grown vegetables on Eden.

Meanwhile, all around her, the air in the tent buzzed with excitement as her colleagues prepared to put their years of research into action. The botanists would begin testing and preparing the soil for crops; the zoologists would begin unfreezing the animal embryos; and the construction team would begin chopping down trees and laying the foundations for apartment complexes. Each member of the crew had their own mission to complete before returning home.

As a chemist, it was Erica's job to travel back and forth to the many bodies of water scattered across the region and add the necessary chemicals to make it potable for human consumption and sustainable for freshwater fish. She had spent the past two years poring over computer diagrams, outlining the size and depths of the waterbodies, and calculating exactly how much base and other chemicals would be needed to bring the much-too-acidic water to their specifications. Today, Erica would be traveling to Zone 1, taking water samples, and beginning to add the human-life-sustaining chemicals.

When she arrived at the first body of water, her exhaustion melted away and she felt exhilarated. She jumped out of the rover, scattering her equipment and canisters of chemicals everywhere. As she kneeled down to test the pH of the water, she flinched. She could swear she saw something move.

She rubbed her eyes, looked again, and jumped a foot into the air. Something was definitely moving. Her heart began to race as she grabbed her scope and submerged it in the water. Her eyes flew open as she stared in disbelief at what she was seeing.

There were electric blue creatures with shining black eyes, long green eels with glowing stripes, and large-headed beings with tentacles crawling on the rocks. The lake was teeming with life, and she could hardly believe she had been the one to discover it.

What a privilege, Erica thought. She tore through her backpack in search of her waterproof camera and danced around the lake, plunging it into the water and taking videos. When the gravity of this discovery hit her, she put her hands to her heart and whispered a prayer of gratitude that she hadn't blindly dumped in the chemicals. The much higher pH would surely have killed off anything living in that water. Erica climbed into the rover and raced back to the ship to speak with the director of Project Eden.

When she arrived at the communications center, Erica burst through the door and immediately uploaded her videos to the computer. Her heart pounded as she composed a letter to the director. Because of the distance from Eden to Earth, it would take seventeen minutes for the message to be received. As she waited, she chewed her fingernails and fantasized how the project director's face would light up when he learned of her discovery. She toyed with the idea that they might name a lake after her. She smiled at the thought. Lake Erica. She liked it.

When the video reply arrived, Erica's hands flew to her mouth. The director of the project and all his cohorts already knew about the indigenous life and were well aware that most of the bodies of water throughout the planet were inhabited. Erica gasped as the director ordered her to do her job and dump the chemicals as directed. It had been determined months ago that the sea creatures were not compatible with the human digestive system, and the director could see no reason to keep them alive. He told her it would be absurd to nurture them when humans needed to utilize the lakes for their own survival.

Erica sat frozen like a statue for what felt like hours before finally preparing a second video. Her normally calm demeanor disappeared, and her eyes became daggers. "What you are suggesting is genocide! We are the aliens on their planet. I will not kill those beautiful creatures. We must come up with another strategy to establish regular drinking water, or we will have to abort this mission.

We can't in good conscience take over a planet that is already inhabited!"

She took a deep breath as angry tears burned her eyes. Her voice calmed.

"Did you even consider that these creatures might be sentient?" she continued. "Please don't ask me to murder these life forms. If you do, I will be forced to include this information in my next press release. The whole world will learn about the monsters that run Project Eden."

Erica sat glued to her chair, refusing to move until she received the next communication. Many hours later, mentally exhausted, she was dozing in her chair when she heard the ping of the computer.

General Donaldson, the director of the project, was on the screen. The sixty-year-old veteran of the center wore an evil sneer on his craggy face. Erica felt her heart drop when he barked, "Erica, you will add the chemicals to the lakes tomorrow as planned and keep your big mouth shut! We have worked for years and spent billions of dollars preparing to develop Eden, and we are not going to let you, of all people, ruin it for everybody!" He brought his face directly up to the camera and snarled, "Oh, and Erica, congratulations on your daughter's new baby. We sincerely hope no harm comes to your new granddaughter."

Erica began gasping for breath as the words of the director sank in. They were threatening her grandchild. Her brain became foggy, and she couldn't get out of her chair. How could she forgive herself if her own granddaughter were harmed? Yet it was against everything she believed in to have any part in the annihilation of all the natural life on this planet.

As Erica paced the floor deep in thought, she prayed to God to guide her, to help her choose the correct thing to do. But this time, she didn't get an answer. Instead, a scenario popped into her head from an ancient *Star Trek* movie. Mr. Spock, with his life hanging in the balance, declared, "The needs of the many outweigh the needs of the few." He was sacrificing his own life to save his crew members, and Erica was ready to do the same. She was fully prepared to risk her own life to save the indigenous species. But it was not her life that was in danger, it was her granddaughter's. Ruining her family was not the kind of sacrifice she was willing to make.

She then thought about Captain Kirk's rebuttal to Mr. Spock. "Sometimes, the needs of the one outweigh the needs of the many." Her granddaughter's safety exceeded all else. Didn't it? But how could she live with herself if she contributed to a genocide?

Erica spent the entire night lying awake in bed, ruminating and softly whimpering. Her friends came over one by one to ask what was wrong, but she told them it was just another headache. The next morning, exhausted and defeated, she walked to the communications center slower than a turtle to propose a compromise that would break her heart.

Still in her nightclothes, her hair stringy and disheveled, she opened up a new message and addressed it to General Donaldson. She proposed that they create a giant aquarium to include every species of life on Eden. Their own personal Noah's Ark. It would be a teaching instrument for children and an entertainment center for families. Marine biologists could come to Eden and study these creatures and give them the honor they deserved. It was the least they could do. Tears ran down her face as she proposed this idea, agreeing to sign their nondisclosure agreement.

The response came back quickly. Director Donaldson said, "Okay, Erica, we will support this plan. The aquarium will be set in Zone 3. The crew will be instructed to disregard the lakes in that area until all the creatures can be removed and relocated to their new enclosures. Meanwhile, you will go ahead with the original plan and drop the chemicals in Zone 1 tomorrow. As we go forward with the aquarium, you will be responsible for the care of the indigenous creatures. You're to remain on Eden permanently and become the spokesperson. All your communications will be monitored. We'll send your supplies and clothing on the next ship." He then smiled and it reminded Erica of the Joker from the Batman movie. "And once again, congratulations on your new grandchild."

Erica watched the video message over and over again, her heart growing heavier with each view. She was never to return to Earth. She would never see her husband or children again. They would never understand why she was not coming home or know about her sacrifice. They would think she valued her job more than her family. She looked at a video of the creatures again and cried. She would have to live with that.

The Cancer Whisperer

They called her the cancer whisperer. She hated that name.

April shifted uncomfortably in her seat and pinched her nose shut. There was a putrid smell wafting through the waiting room, and her face turned crimson as her stomach began to churn. When the medical assistant called her name, she jumped up and power-walked to the doctor's office.

As she strolled in, Dr. Turner smiled and said, "What brings you here today, April?"

April took a seat next to the ear, nose, and throat doctor. She looked at the floor and whispered, "Dr. Turner, I know you're going to think I'm crazy, but ever since I had COVID, I'm pretty sure I can smell cancer. You know, like those cancer-sniffing dogs."

If this had been the year 2019, Dr. Turner might have sent April for a psych consult, but over the past few years, he had seen hundreds of patients with all sorts of bizarre taste and smell distortions post-COVID-19 infection. He wasn't ruling anything out.

"What makes you think that?" he asked.

"Well, when I had COVID three years ago, I lost my senses of taste and smell…"

Dr. Turner interrupted, "That's called anosmia."

"Yes, Doc, I know. Then a few weeks later, I began smelling smoke all day long."

"That's called phantosmia."

April furrowed her brows. "Yes, I know. Then about a year later, I began to smell and taste certain things again, but nothing was right. My coffee tasted like raw sewage, my pizza tasted like overcooked brussels sprouts, and my husband smelled like pine needles."

"That's called parosmia."

"Yes, Doctor, I know." Tears burned her eyes as she begged, "Please help me. I just want to be normal again." She stared at the floor. "Here's the thing, Doc. My mother-in-law has breast cancer, and even before her diagnosis, she smelled as if she'd been sprayed by a skunk. Nobody else smelled it. When I took her to see her oncologist, every other patient in the office smelled like skunk. It was awful. And your waiting room smells pretty bad, too. Does the woman sitting there have cancer?"

Dr. Turner opened the door and peeked out. "Yes, April, she does." Intrigued, he said, "If you don't mind, let's take a walk upstairs to the mammography center and check this out."

April's heart pounded as she entered the waiting room of the mammography center, worried people would stare at her. When she realized most of the women were paying attention to their phones, it gave her courage. She began nonchalantly walking around the room, sniffing as quietly as she could.

She turned to Dr. Turner. "The one in the red shirt, and the one in the blue pantsuit. Both skunks."

Dr. Turner excused himself to speak to the radiologist. She promised to send him a report. When they got back to his office, the doctor examined April's nose and throat very carefully. As with all his other post-COVID patients who had lost their senses, there was little to recommend. April had already tried intensive smell training, but after three years, it was doubtful anything would help.

The doctor was just about to propose to April that they

experiment with a course of decongestants when something occurred to him, and he thought, *Would it even be in April's best interest to get rid of this awesome talent?*

He began thinking about the new pathways in research that could open up, and how many lives she could potentially save. He then suppressed a smile as he imagined his name being prominently featured in medical journals.

Soon after April left his office, Dr. Turner got the call from the radiologist. April had been correct; both women had cancer. The radiologist told Dr. Turner that she had almost missed one of the tumors because it was so small, but thanks to his warning, she'd rechecked the mammogram and found it. Early stage 1 cancer. The woman would be fine.

Dr. Turner grinned as he wrote in his journal, *Day 1: One life saved.*

The next day, he canceled all his afternoon appointments and arranged a meeting with some of his colleagues. When he called April to invite her as the guest of honor, she said, "Doc, thanks for thinking of me, but I don't want to come. I hate being the center of attention, and I'm afraid I'll have a panic attack."

Dr. Turner promised there would be no pressure. He told her to just think about it as a small group of friends getting together for lunch. What convinced her to come was when Dr. Turner assured her that her best hope for a cure was if a team of doctors worked on her case together.

When she finally agreed, April asked, "Is it okay if I bring my toddler? It's too late to call a babysitter."

The next day, April arrived at the conference room, panting and out of breath. She was struggling to balance a squirming toddler in one arm and the heavy diaper bag in the other. Dr. Turner jumped up to help her and introduced her to the other guests. April looked around nervously and stammered a greeting as she plopped Sammy onto the carpet with some toys.

The doctors had catered an expensive lunch, and one of them turned to her and said, "April, this is for you. Have anything you want."

April frowned. She felt insulted. "You did this for me? You know I can't taste anything. That's why I'm here. I can't even remember what foods taste like anymore. I've been so depressed."

She bent down to give Sammy a couple of cookies and kept an eye on him as he happily consumed his special treats. When she and Sammy were settled in, Dr. Turner turned to April and asked her to start from the beginning.

As she began explaining her symptoms, she noticed a couple of the doctors were sniggering. Her face turned crimson as her voice broke. "I knew none of you would believe me!" she cried.

Dr. Turner jumped up. "We're not laughing at you, April. It just happens that there's a very unpleasant odor coming from the direction of your toddler. It's kind of like a gift that you can't smell it."

All the doctors laughed as April's eyes flared. "You think that's funny? I often can't tell when Sammy has a dirty diaper. One time, he developed such a bad rash he needed medicine for a week." She tossed the changing pad onto the floor and proceeded to change Sammy's diaper right there in the room, smiling at her small act of revenge.

After spending an hour in the conference room, the doctors wanted to see April in action. They accompanied her to the mammography center and carefully watched her sniff around. Dr. Turner discreetly videotaped her, and the radiologist again confirmed her correct diagnoses.

Later that day, after April went home, the conference room

thrummed with excitement as the doctors debated how to best use her talents. Should she work in hospitals with difficult-to-diagnose patients, radiography centers, and low-income clinics? Would it be ethical to tell people on the street they had cancer? Would it be ethical to not tell them? There were many decisions to be made.

Over the next few days, April was a guinea pig as the research team poked and prodded her. She was examined from head to toe, including MRIs and a CT scan. Nothing abnormal stood out. The doctors were baffled.

As the research team discussed how to best use April's talents, they hired her to work in their own medical facility. They had her divide her time between the mammography center, their colonoscopy suite, and their low-income clinic. April found her new job to be very uncomfortable and insisted on carrying a large clipboard that she could hide behind. The only thing she was excited about was her work in the clinic. Though she was only there one day a week, she was proud to help people who might not be able to afford diagnostic tests. She sniffed out cancer in people whose silent disease might have gone undetected until it was too late.

After a few months of things going smoothly, April woke one morning, turned on the news, and discovered she was the lead story. Somebody from the research team must have leaked her name. People were immediately fascinated by her ability, and she began receiving invitations to be a guest on all the morning news programs. The producers wanted her to sniff the news anchors on the air as if she were a dog.

Dr. Turner knew how anxious April was to speak in public but still encouraged her to embrace the publicity, arguing that they could raise more money for research. "Think of all the people you could help." It was what he always said. He promised April he would always be at her side and would do most of the talking. She refused. She was already beginning to develop an anxiety disorder from all the attention. So Dr. Turned accepted the invitations on her behalf. With April's permission, he showed videos of her at work, and now people knew her face as well as her talent.

With all the unwanted publicity, April received an invitation from the White House. The president wanted to meet the woman who was saving lives with her nose. Though she wasn't sure how she would get through it, she accepted on behalf of her husband. She understood how many sacrifices he was making and how his whole life had been upended, as well. Besides, her mother told her she would kill her if she turned it down.

When they arrived at the White House, April grasped onto her husband as if he were a life raft. She trembled when she shook hands with the president, and her eye began to twitch when she discovered the First Lady smelled like a skunk. It took every ounce of her courage to whisper it to the president's wife, who made an emergency appointment with her doctor. When she received her diagnosis, it was the top news story for a week. It was then that the media dubbed April "the Cancer Whisperer."

As she became more recognizable, April's eye twitch became permanent. She felt anxious and frazzled every single day and began taking antidepressants. She felt like she was living in a pressure cooker and didn't know how much longer she could keep it up.

Then one morning, something remarkable happened. April woke up and her coffee tasted like coffee, her breakfast cereal tasted sweet, and her pregnancy test came out positive. She called Dr. Turner immediately.

"Come to my office right away," he told her.

When April arrived, she noticed the doctor was sweating. He sat her down and had her smell several essential oils and discovered her senses of taste and smell were definitely coming back. When he asked about her husband's mother, she told him, "It's wonderful not having to retch when your mother-in-law is in the room."

Dr. Turner didn't know how to feel. On the one hand, he was joyous that his favorite patient was returning to normal. On the other hand, April was losing her ability to sniff out cancer. She was losing her ability to help people, and he was losing his best research subject.

He suspected this might happen if she became pregnant, but he wasn't prepared for it to happen so soon. April's body had begun repairing itself and returning to normal. His mind raced as he tried to come up with solutions.

"April, maybe I can do something to help," he said.

She furrowed her brows. "Doc, I hoped you'd be happy for me. I am beginning to feel like myself again. For the first time in a very long time, I was actually able to enjoy food again and smell my toddler's sweet head. It was amazing. Why would you want to take that away?"

Dr. Turner stood and rocked back on his heels. He took April's hand. "You've helped so many people. Are you sure you want to give that up so that you can taste some pizza? Your amazing gift has saved lives. You're a hero."

April put her head in her hands and sniffled. "Don't you think this is torturing me? But I don't want to take my meds while I'm pregnant. And yes, I know exactly what I'm losing. I've also been miserable for such a long time." She looked up and dried her tears. "Listen, I've spoken with my clergyman, and he told me it's not my obligation to do something that can harm me, either mentally or physically." She took a deep breath and asked, "Besides, what could we do to stop it?"

"I've been experimenting with a procedure that might be able to reverse your new gains," Dr. Turner said. "I can do it right in my office."

April frowned at the thought of minor surgery. "If I have the procedure, can you guarantee that I'll still be able to smell cancer?"

Dr. Turner looked at the floor. "No, April. The procedure is experimental. It would reinjure the neurons in your nose, and we would hope the regeneration brought the same results. It's impossible to predict if it would work."

"If I don't regain the ability to sniff cancer after the procedure, would my smell and taste eventually return to normal?"

"I don't know. We've only done this procedure on mice. It might take away your senses for good."

April sighed. "Would you be willing to have the same procedure so we'd be in the same boat? It seems fair."

Dr. Turner closed his eyes and steepled his fingers. The room was silent as doctor and patient remained deep in thought. Finally, he said, "Why would you ask me to do that, April? I will never have the ability to sniff out cancer. I could never do what you do."

April shook her head. "That's what I thought." She hesitated a moment and added, "I'm in the process of writing a book, which I'm calling *The Cancer Whisperer: Gift or Burden*. I'd like to include you in the book. Is that okay?"

Dr. Turner wrinkled his forehead. "What are you going to say about me? You know what I care about most is that together, we saved lives. I hope you're going to say what great work we've done, and how I helped you become a hero for so many people."

April looked at Dr. Turner with tears in her eyes. "The stress is killing me, Doc, and I can't have that while I'm pregnant. Maybe the pregnancy is why my senses have returned so suddenly. Maybe not, but either way, no more tests. This year has been hellish for me, and I'm moving out of town with my family. Please don't try to make me feel guilty for wanting to be able to smell my new baby's head, and yes, to even taste pizza again. I just want to be normal, and I don't think that's too much to ask."

Dr. Turner smiled sadly, knowing that he'd lost this fight. "I wish you and your family the best of luck," he said. "I'm delighted you're regaining your senses and am proud of the work we've done together. You have my full permission to include me in your book, and I'll be the first in line at Barnes and Noble to buy it. If you have any questions, please don't hesitate to call. Best of luck with the new baby."

April stood on her tiptoes and whispered in his ear, "There's going to be a picture of me in the book sniffing the First Lady. That's because of you. I met the president and the First Lady because of our work together, and although it was a terrifying experience, I'll always be grateful." She kissed Dr. Turner on the cheek. "Thanks for everything, Doc. It's been surreal."

Tears burned his eyes as he closed the door behind her.

The Most Delicious Turkey Leg

Marianne first saw it on *Alfred Hitchcock Presents*. A woman hit her philandering husband in the head with a frozen leg of lamb, killed him, and later served the meat to the police, obliterating all the evidence.

She thought about it as she scrutinized her lazy husband sitting in front of the TV with a beer in his hand, his belly hanging over his lap, and halitosis so bad it could choke a skunk. She pondered nineteen long years of being called fat, dumb, and useless. As she walked into the kitchen to defrost something for dinner, she wondered if the frozen turkey leg would work as well as the leg of lamb.

It did.

The Doll with the
Creepy Glass Eyes

"Oh, but they're so cute. Can't I take just one? Please, Jake?"

Jake shuddered as he looked at Zoe's collection of porcelain dolls. He could swear their creepy glass eyes were following him wherever he went. He had to admit, though, that Zoe did an artful job of organizing them in their ornate glass showcase.

The top shelf displayed the tall fashionistas with their elegant gowns and stylish hats. Next came the baby dolls, adorable and realistic in their newborn onesies. Then the miniatures, tiny and delicate. And finally, the Disney princesses, the dolls that had gotten Zoe excited about collecting in the first place.

"Zoe," Jake asked, "how many dolls do you have?"

She furrowed her brows, deep in thought. "Well, let's see. I've collected two a year since I was five, so around forty dolls." She turned to her boyfriend, pouting. "Jake, I'll be happy if I can take just one."

"You know your porcelain dolls give me the heebie-jeebies. They're so creepy! Look, I'm not proud I have pediophobia, but I just do."

"Pediophobia? Is that even a real thing?"

"Yes, Zoe. My fear of dolls is real. I developed the phobia after my brother took me to see the Chucky movie when I was six. I had nightmares for months. So how about you leave your dolls at your parents' house and you can visit them whenever you go there?"

Zoe's chin began to quiver as she made her final plea. "How about this instead? I'll just take my Anne of Green Gables doll. Look how cute she is with her little red braids and her little green pinafore dress and her little straw hat. My grandma bought her from a shaman on a small island in Canada, and it was the last gift she ever gave me. Can't I take just this one?"

Jake sighed. How could he say no? Zoe was the love of his life, and he was so happy she had finally agreed to move in with him. Plus, she never complained about how much space his baseball collection took up, so how could he deny her that one doll? He would just have to suck it up and deal with it.

"Okay," he said, "but please don't put it anywhere that I can see it at night. By the way, I'm glad you picked the Anne doll. She really is the least creepy of all your dolls."

Zoe planted kisses all over Jake's face. Together they packed up the rest of her belongings, and she officially moved in with him. When Zoe walked into their bedroom, she told Jake, "I'm putting my Anne doll on my night table behind the lamp. You won't even be able to see her."

Jake glanced over and saw just a tiny bit of red hair sticking out from behind one side of the lamp. He felt fine. This doll was not going to be a problem at all.

The next morning, Jake woke up to the smell of fresh coffee and blueberry muffins. He jumped out of bed with a huge grin on his face. Having Zoe move in was the best idea he'd ever had.

After breakfast, Zoe left for work, and Jake started setting up his workstation at the kitchen table. Ever since the pandemic had begun, he'd been working from home, and he enjoyed not having to commute.

Just as he was opening his computer, he began to hear a voice, in singsong fashion, coming from the bedroom. It sounded like the voice was saying, "Oh Ja-ake, Jakey-poo…come on in here, handsome."

His first thought was that Zoe had forgotten to turn the radio off before she left. Or perhaps it was the Echo Dot responding to a perceived question. He crept into the bedroom very slowly and heard the voice again.

"Hey, handsome, thanks for picking me to come to live with you. You made the right choice. Those other dolls are so boring. I waited years for someone like you to come along, so don't worry, Jakey-poo. I'll do whatever it takes for us to be together."

Jake's heart began hammering in his chest. The voice was coming from the doll. He raced out of the room and called Zoe. "What the hell is wrong with your doll? You didn't tell me it was a talking doll. Is this a joke? It's not funny! In fact, a heart attack would be funnier than this."

Zoe wrinkled her forehead in confusion. "What are you talking about? I don't have any talking dolls. Just close the bedroom door, and we'll discuss this when I get home." She was becoming alarmed. She hadn't realized Jake's phobia was so severe, and she made a mental note to look up therapists when she got home. The thought crossed her mind that maybe she didn't know Jake as well as she thought.

After speaking with Zoe, Jake went out for a run to clear his head. When he came home, the house was silent. He spent the rest of the day trying to convince himself that he'd imagined the whole thing, but part of him was worried he was becoming unhinged.

That night, as Zoe was getting ready for bed, Jake heard a loud scream. He raced into the bedroom and saw Zoe sitting on the floor with a bloody foot. "Jake!" she yelled. "One of the tacks from your bulletin board was on the floor, and I stepped on it! Get me some antibiotic cream and a Band-Aid. You need to be more careful not to drop those tacks. It really hurts."

Jake came back with the Band-Aids and took a quick peek at the doll. No, it couldn't possibly have been her.

The next morning, Zoe told Jake she had buried Anne at the bottom of her sock drawer. Her foot hurt, and she was feeling annoyed, so left in a huff. She hoped hiding the doll would put an end to Jake's irrational fear.

Jake climbed out of bed in a sour mood, mad that Zoe had left early. He dragged himself to the kitchen and poured a cup of coffee. As he was taking his first sip, he heard the voice again.

"Jake, get me out of this sock drawer! I'm so cramped in here. I can barely breathe."

Jake's breathing became ragged, and though he put his hands over his ears, he still couldn't block it out.

"Hey," the voice continued, "how did you like that thing I did to Zoe last night? Pretty good, huh? Tonight, there'll be another surprise. I love you, Jakey. Soon, we'll be together, just the two of us."

Jake was now dizzy, and his heart was racing. If this was some kind of joke, he would have to ask Zoe to move out. He packed up his computer and went straight to his parents' house for the day. He was sweaty and agitated when he arrived and told his mother he needed a break from his own apartment.

She said, "I told you it was too soon to ask Zoe to move in with you."

At the end of the day, Jake drove to their apartment and waited in his car until Zoe came home. As she got out of her car, he ran up to her and stammered, "I know I said you could keep Anne, but please get rid of that doll. She's so creepy! I feel like I'm losing my mind. I promise I'll go to that therapist we talked about last night if you just get rid of that devil doll."

Zoe nodded in agreement. "Okay. I didn't realize how much it bothered you. I'll bring the doll back to my parents' house this weekend, I promise."

Jake gave Zoe a grateful smile, and together they sat down to dinner. Shortly after they finished eating, Jake heard a loud crash in the bedroom. He ran in and saw Zoe sitting on the floor, holding her ankle. She bellowed, "Jake, how did the floor get wet? I could have killed myself slipping in that puddle!"

Jake sputtered, "It wasn't me. Zoe, I think it was Anne. I swear it wasn't me. I don't know how she did it, but it was her!"

"Just get me some ice for my ankle," Zoe growled. "You're really scaring me, Jake. You can sleep on the couch tonight."

The next morning, Zoe left early again. Jake decided it would be too stressful to work from home, so as soon as Zoe left, he put on his noise-canceling headphones, turned on some music, and cranked the volume up high. Instead of music, what he heard was, "Good morning, handsome. I'm getting tired of the sock drawer. Please get me out. Great news. My plan for getting rid of Zoe is working. Tonight will be the *pièce de résistance.*"

He ripped the headphones off his ears and tossed them out the window. He ran out of his house without his computer or jacket and drove to his parents' house. He was shaking so badly when he arrived that his mother took him straight to the emergency room. The psychiatrist on call wrote him a prescription for anti-anxiety medication and recommended he begin therapy two times a week. She cautiously let him go home and told him to call immediately if he had any more hallucinations.

When Zoe received the message from Jake's mother, she left work early to be with him. "I'm so sorry I didn't listen to you," she told him. "I don't care about that stupid doll. I promise I'll do whatever it takes to help you feel better. I thought you were just playing a joke on me to get rid of my doll."

That night, as Zoe was getting into bed, Jake heard a scream. He couldn't take much more of this. He darted out of the bathroom in a panic, yelling, "Zoe, what's wrong? What did Anne do to you this time?"

He looked down and saw Zoe lying in bed in a pool of blood with a knife sticking out of her thigh.

"Jake," she screamed, "what's wrong with you? Why would you put a knife in the bed? You could have killed me! Get me to the hospital, I'm going to need stitches!" Then she added, "I'm sorry, Jake, I don't think us living together is working out. I'm going to move back home tomorrow. Don't worry, I'll take Anne with me!"

Just as Zoe was breaking his heart, they both heard a voice bellowing from the sock drawer. It said, "No! I don't want to go home with you, Zoe. I want to stay with Jake. I love Jake! I will do anything to be with him, even if I have to kill you! Go home, Zoe. Jake and I don't want you."

Jake's face turned crimson as the adrenaline soared through his body. In a fit of rage, he grabbed Anne out of the sock drawer and screamed, "You will never hurt Zoe again!"

He began to bash the doll's head against the floor, slamming it over and over again until her porcelain head and body were nothing more than shards of glass. He got the broom and swept every piece of her into a bag and put it in the garbage bin outside. Then he set it on fire and watched it burn, making sure there was nothing left of Anne but ashes.

As he carried Zoe to the car to go to the hospital, they heard a low moan coming from the garbage. "Help me, Jake, I love you, I love you…"

In the emergency room, Zoe received twelve stitches, and that night she and Jake slept in a hotel. They both took the next couple of weeks off from work, staying at Jake's parents' house. When they felt ready, they moved back home, determined to look for a new apartment. Both Zoe and Jake had PTSD, and it would take a long time for them to feel normal again. The worst part was that they couldn't even tell anybody what had happened. Who would believe them? They sounded insane.

As things began to normalize, Zoe returned to work, and Jake cautiously set up his workstation in his home office. He slowly opened up his computer, relieved not to hear any voices coming from the bedroom.

As he began reading his emails, he was shocked to see one that didn't have a sender. He tentatively opened it up. There, attached to the email, was a video. A video of Anne.

"Hey, handsome," she said. "You can't get rid of me that easily. Oh, silly Jake, you made it so much harder for us to be together. Don't worry, though. I'll figure it out."

Mission in Time

Having a tracker implanted in your arm was optional, but if you wanted to time travel, it was mandatory. I had avoided trackers my whole life, but once I had one put in, I saw the advantages; I was able to program my self-driving car with a flick of my wrist.

Though I felt a bit paranoid having this device inside of my body, I was well aware that anxiety was a small price to pay to be able to travel through time. The fact was, the Bureau of Time Travel limited your trip to two hours, and they needed a way to keep tabs on you if you exceeded your cutoff. Hence, the tracker.

The biggest problem with time travel, and the thing that made my blood boil, was that it was only available to the billionaires who funded the project. Kind of like trips into space were in the early twenty-first century. I often felt furious that I worked all those hours of overtime just to provide entertainment for the elite. That's why I didn't feel too guilty about what I had to do to finagle a golden ticket for myself.

Plus, I felt like I deserved it. I had spent the past five years neglecting my family and pouring my lifeblood into the time travel project. Not only that, but I was the one who perfected the boomerang coil, the device that creates the loop that allows people to return home. Not that I'm boasting, but without that, you'd be stuck in the future. Anyway, I kept my discovery hostage until the

Bureau agreed to let me travel. I'm not usually the kind of person that takes advantage of situations, and I felt sick to my stomach knowing I was jeopardizing my good relationship with my boss, but I had an urgent matter to take care of in the future and I couldn't trust anyone else to do it.

After word got out about my contribution to time travel, the Bureau arranged a lot of interviews. I was happy to do them. It allowed me to be home for dinner every night and spend time with my family.

The question I got asked most was, "Why can't we travel to the past?"

People always got mad when I told them it was impossible. They couldn't seem to wrap their heads around the idea that time travel was only in one direction. The Bureau actually got a lot of hate mail. Yes, it was unfortunate that we couldn't go back and prevent World War III, but I just wished people could appreciate the fact that maybe we could stop a war from happening in the future.

As the development of time travel became a reality, the Bureau got to work creating many new laws and limitations. With so many unscrupulous people in the world, a mandatory prison sentence of twenty years was established for any person who took advantage of travel for their own monetary gain. A team of special agents was commissioned to monitor the financial activity of each and every traveler as well as that of their families for many years after their return.

Of course, my reason for traveling had nothing to do with profit. As I worked to perfect the boomerang coil, I often dreamed of all the wonderful things I could see. All the new technology, the new discoveries, and all the things my children and future grandchildren would have accomplished with their lives. The idea was intoxicating. But there was one thing in particular I had to do, and my mind was set on it.

I tossed and turned the night before the trip, getting out of bed early so I wouldn't disturb my husband. With my adrenaline buzzing, I paced back and forth in the living room until it was time to get dressed. I put a lot of thought into what to wear and decided on a classic black business suit in the hopes I wouldn't stick out. I then went to my jewelry box and plucked out my Star of David necklace for good luck. The pendant, studded with rubies and tiny pearls, was a treasured gift from my grandmother. Feeling it around my neck always made me feel calmer.

After getting dressed, I snuck into my home office and removed a small package from a locked desk drawer. I carefully placed it in my backpack, zipped it up, and headed to the kitchen to have breakfast with my family. As I walked in, I smiled at my husband, who was already at the stove cooking eggs as my two little boys chased each other in circles. They were wearing their matching Superman pajamas and playing superhero versus the villain. They were so cute I had to take a video.

My husband smirked, "Good morning, time traveler," and handed me a plate with a freshly made spinach and cheese omelet on it. It was my favorite, and it smelled so good, but I couldn't eat much because my stomach was full of guilt. I had never lied to my husband about anything important before, but I couldn't tell him the truth about my reason for traveling.

With shame burning my throat, I drew him into a long embrace and told him I loved him. As I did, I reached down and snuck a sealed envelope into his pocket just in case I didn't come back. Next, I called over my boys. They climbed onto my lap and I squeezed them in a bear hug until they squirmed and complained.

My four-year-old hopped down and asked, "Mommy, are you

going to work? When are you coming back? Can we have pizza for lunch?"

Tears stung my eyes as I crossed my fingers and promised Mommy would be home soon. I really hoped I was coming back. It would break my heart to leave them.

Though I usually took the car to work, I decided to walk to the travel center instead. It was only a couple of miles away, and I needed time to think. As I got closer, cortisol began to pour through my veins like water from a faucet. My feelings were a mixture of exhilaration, excitement, and sheer terror.

I was traveling thirty years into the future. No one had traveled that far before, and I didn't know what to expect. The possibilities were endless. Perhaps there had been a World War IV or another pandemic, or maybe the Earth had been hit by a meteor and I was traveling into an abyss.

By the time I walked into the building, I was drenched in sweat and my breathing was ragged. I scanned my tracker at the entryway, and a guard checked my backpack for weapons. Afterward, I went directly to the vault, where I was greeted by my young colleague, Dr. Vargas.

She smiled at me and crooned, "Good morning, Dr. Feldman. You're right on time. As requested, the machine has been set to March 8th, 2102. You will have two hours exactly. Please set the timer on your tracker." She looked up and grinned. "Have a safe trip, Dr. Feldman, and when you get back, I want to hear every single detail. I'm so jealous. Don't leave anything out."

After stepping into the time pod, I began to shake so badly that I had trouble pressing the start button. As the pod sprang to life, I felt like I was free-falling, as if I were skydiving from 20,000 feet in the air. I was dizzy and nauseated and grabbed onto the sidebars and shut my eyes tight.

Just when I thought I couldn't take it any longer, the vehicle lurched to a halt and the doors popped open. I stepped out very slowly and was immediately greeted by an android in a blue jumpsuit. Now *that* was interesting. The Bureau had never employed androids before.

It said, "Greetings, Dr. Feldman, we've been waiting for you."

My jaw dropped as I looked around. I was no longer inside a vault with just one time machine; rather, I was in a room the size of a gymnasium with about thirty time pods. They were thin and sleek and much more advanced than the one I'd come in. I'll bet nobody felt like they were free-falling in those vehicles.

My mouth continued to hang open while I watched people getting in and out of the pods as if time travel was as commonplace as driving a car. I had so many questions buzzing through my brain, and it practically killed me that I had only enough time for a few.

I put my hands on the droid's shoulders to steady myself and asked, "Is time travel still limited to two hours? Are we still at the same location as the original vault?"

The droid removed my hands from its shoulders and responded, "Dr. Feldman, travel time can extend up to twenty-four hours per trip now, but only under special circumstances. Let's say you have been diagnosed with a fatal condition, and your child's wedding is coming up in a couple of years. We would allow you to travel ahead and stay for the entirety of the event. We have a whole new guidebook of special rules and regulations. Meanwhile, I am sorry to tell you that you are still limited to two hours. The duration of time travel will not increase for another ten years from your time. And yes, we are still located on Broad Street and Elm. We've just expanded a bit."

With no time to waste, I headed to the exit, where I was handed a jet pack with instructions to maintain a height of thirty feet above ground until I got to my destination. My head buzzed with excitement as I slipped on the jet pack. I couldn't believe it. My lab had just started developing the technology, and now I was seeing it in all its glory. I pondered whether I had somehow played a role in its advancement and made a mental note to return a little early to check the inner controls.

With my jet pack strapped in place, I told the GPS where I wanted to go, and I was soon on my way. When I realized I would arrive at my destination in under ten minutes, my whole body tingled with excitement. I would have time to complete my mission, with enough time left over to study the jet pack's construction.

After a short, exhilarating ride, I touched down gently at the Johnson Memory Care Center and breathed in a sigh of relief that it was still there. I dropped off my jet pack with an attendant and went straight to the front desk to ask for the room number for Ava Feldman.

The receptionist checked her computer and then checked it again. She told me I was not on the list of visitors for this patient. I asked her to please call over the nursing home director, having memorized a number of excuses why she should let me in, but I didn't need it.

The director took one look at me and smiled. "Wow, the resemblance between you and Miss Ava is uncanny. You must be her daughter." She furrowed her brows. "That's funny, I thought Miss Ava only had sons."

I smiled back. "Don't worry about the error, it's not your fault. I've been out of the country."

When I spotted Ava, she was sitting in a wheelchair gazing blankly out the window. I was startled at how poorly she looked, and the lump that formed in my throat threatened to gag me. Her once luxurious brown hair was now gray and cut very short. She had no muscle tone, and her sparkling green eyes were now dull and vacant.

I forced a smile. "Good morning, Ava. How are you today?"

She looked up and asked, "Do I know you?" She stared at my necklace. "I think I have the same necklace."

I took her hand. "Yes, Ava, you did. You gave it to me. Don't you recognize me?"

She shut her eyes in deep concentration, digging for a lost memory. She finally responded. "No, but I think I have been waiting for you."

I let go of her hand and pulled off my backpack. I unzipped it and took out a bag of Oreo cookies. As I held the bag in my hands, I suddenly froze like a statue, momentarily struck by what I was about to do. I rubbed my necklace for courage, took a breath, and placed five of the cookies on a napkin in her lap.

"Go ahead and eat them, honey," I said, smiling. "I brought them especially for you."

Ava beamed as she began eating the cookies. "I think these are my favorites."

"Yes," I said, "mine too."

Ava ate the cookies with gusto, crumbs flying out of her mouth as she moaned, "Mmmmm," over and over again. Despite the spittle hitting my face, I pulled my chair close to her and began telling her a story. I knew she wouldn't understand it, but I felt compelled. I took a deep breath and began.

"Ava, do you remember when your father was diagnosed with early-onset Alzheimer's disease? Even though you were scared, you decided to get tested to see if you'd inherited the defective gene. Well, when you tested positive, you put a plan in place. I'm your plan." I looked at the floor. "I had really hoped Alzheimer's would have been cured by now and we wouldn't need it."

Ava wet her fingers to pick up the last few crumbs and began begging for more cookies. There were a few left, so I passed them over to her. As she twisted the chocolatey top off the cookie and began licking the cream, I continued my story.

"You never wanted to be a burden to your family the way your father was, so you wrote a living will. You asked your family to check you into the Johnson Memory Care Center as soon as you could no longer take care of yourself."

I pulled a piece of paper out of my backpack and showed it to her.

"Look," I said. "You wrote me a letter and asked for my help." A lump came to my throat as I mumbled, "I'm sorry I couldn't get here sooner."

Ava finished the last of her cookies and began tapping her head. I could see she was on the cusp of remembering something but couldn't quite grasp it. She became very agitated, shouting, "Who are you? Who are you?" louder and louder until the nurse came running in and asked me to leave.

"I'm sorry," the nurse said, "but I can't let you stay when Ava gets agitated like this. Don't worry, though, I'll call your dad and ask him to come right away. He can always get Ava to calm down."

I clutched my heart and trudged out the door, turning once to blow Ava a kiss. I burst into sobs, crying openly as I programmed the jet pack for my return to the travel center. I had accomplished everything I set out to do.

When I arrived back at the vault, I dried my tears and exited the pod. Dr. Vargas asked if I'd had a good trip, and I just nodded. I told her I was too exhausted to talk but would tell her all about it the next day. I needed time to weave a story.

You see, I always knew Ava wouldn't want to live that way. So I laced her cookies with poison. She would be dead by now. I didn't worry about being arrested because it wasn't going to happen for another thirty years.

I walked very slowly from the time travel center to my house, pondering everything that had happened. I wondered: *Would it be called a homicide because I did, in fact, murder another human being? Or would it be called suicide?*

Either way, for the first time in a long while, I felt light as a feather. As I strolled down the street, I pulled out my phone and called my husband.

"Hi honey, it's me, Ava. I'm on the way home. I'll pick up the pizza." I took a breath and whispered, "I love you so much."

The Apodalypse

Charlotte's face lit up when she spotted her two best friends waiting for her at a lunch table at the senior center. She walked over, gave them each a hug, and said, "It's so good to see you. I missed you guys so much."

Pearl pulled out the chair for Charlotte, who sat down gingerly, not yet used to her new hip. After arranging her purse and cardigan on the back of her chair, she said, "Please, ladies, fill me in on what's been happening in the world. My iPhone was stolen in rehab, and I haven't been able to listen to the news for more than a month. You know how much I hate to be uninformed. It's been killing me."

Pearl and Esther looked at each other and smiled. They had some juicy news to share with Charlotte, and they knew exactly how she would react. The three best friends loved a good debate, and Pearl and Esther tingled with excitement in anticipation of the one that was about to begin.

"I'll start," Pearl smirked. She looked at her friend and said, "I have one word for you: Apodalypse."

Charlotte frowned. "You mean apocalypse? Are you having a senior moment?"

"No," sneered Pearl, offended by what her friend was insinuating. "That is actually what the news media is calling it. The Apodalypse. It's a stupid name for an even crazier story. Anyway, listen up, because this is a good one. Last month, six of the richest men in the world paid a billion dollars each to take a two-week joy ride into space. A billion dollars to sit in a pod the size of a small recreational vehicle, just so they could call themselves astronauts." Pearl's jaw clenched as she continued. "We're eating this disgusting boxed lunch in a senior center because we can't survive on our Social Security, and those men paid a billion dollars each for two weeks of fun."

"Pearl" snapped Charlotte. "Please, let's not have another diatribe about how the government doesn't care about senior citizens. We all know how you feel. Just finish the story."

"Well," piped in Ester, "Pearl's not wrong. The government doesn't care about seniors." She took a bite of her mealy meatloaf to prove it and threw down her fork. "Yuck!" She turned to Charlotte. "Pearl's getting too emotional, so I'll tell the rest of the story. Okay, so while these billionaires were busy having their little fun, their space shuttle got caught up in the gravitational pull of the star Exotica, and now their pod is revolving around the star in an endless loop. Just like how the earth revolves around the sun. They can't break free of the star's gravity. They'll be circling the star forever."

"Oh, my God," exclaimed Charlotte. "Those poor men." She closed her eyes for a minute, trying to picture it in her head. "How are they not burning up being so close to a star? How are they still alive? Does NASA have a plan to get them home?" She took a breath. "We have to help them."

"You're such a bleeding heart," said Esther. "Don't worry. Exotica is a dead star, so it no longer gives off any heat. And as for the cold, well, their shuttle is well insulated. They are just fine and dandy. By the way, want to know which six guys are up there? Which six guys wasted billions of dollars just for a little fun?"

At first, Charlotte shook her head no, but when she saw how anxious her friends were to share the news, she sighed, "Okay, go ahead."

With a big grin spreading across her face, Esther said, "Great. Let's see if you still have sympathy after I tell you who they are. Are you ready? Number one is Ellsworth Muscrat III. Then comes B.F. Jeffries, Colin Eagen Smith, Vidyot Singh, Vladimir Alexander Petrov, and Yong-saeng Kim. Still feeling that sympathy? Cause I'm not."

Charlotte furrowed her eyebrows and asked, "Is Vladimir the Russian oligarch who lives in London?" She then shook her head. "No, no, no, you won't get me to change my mind about how I feel. Even if I don't like them or agree with anything they say or do, the fact is it's their money and they are entitled to spend it any way they choose. But more importantly, they are human beings just like us, and for that reason alone, they deserve to be helped."

Pearl looked at the floor and muttered under her breath, "Oh, they are definitely not like us."

As Charlotte began absently cutting up her meatloaf, her eyes suddenly flew open and she exclaimed, "Oh, my gosh, what are they going to do for oxygen and food and water?"

"It's not a problem," said Pearl. "They have a water reclaimer on board, so as long as they continue to pee, they will have enough water to drink. Same for the oxygen. It's being recycled."

"Eww," said Charlotte.

"Plus," continued Pearl, "they have enough food to last for two years."

"But what about after that?" groaned Charlotte. "They'll starve. What a horrible way to die."

"Would you please stop worrying?" shouted Pearl. "Our government is currently pouring billions of our tax dollars into figuring out a way to send a supply shuttle to dock with their pod. They have all the most brilliant mathematicians and scientists working on it. Twenty-four hours a day, our country is spending our money to keep these billionaires alive. Meanwhile, thankfully, at least nobody else will be put in danger. It has been determined that it is too risky to send a rescue mission, so at least they are being reasonable about that."

Esther started laughing. "Just think about it. Six of the bossiest bosses in the world, used to living in luxury, stuck together in one tiny place with nobody to serve them. They have to wash their own dishes, clean their own toilets, and worst of all, they have to get along with each other. Could you imagine the fighting that must be going on in that pod?"

"But the best part is," laughed Esther, "they all share one very tiny bathroom, and they're running out of toilet paper."

"You think that's funny?" barked Charlotte.

"Oh," said Pearl and Esther in unison, "we think it's hilarious."

Donning a mischievous grin, Pearl said, "Charlotte, I'm about to tell you something that I think is going to dissolve your sympathy for these men like sugar in a cup of scorching hot tea."

Charlotte shook her head. "I doubt it."

"Oh, yeah?" said Pearl. "Well, listen to this. It seems that these billionaires have a toilet that collects their bowel movements in a non-recyclable plastic container, and when they flush, it shoots it into space. They are literally shooting their poop into space and polluting the final frontier. There are actual photos of plastic containers following their pod in the same endless revolution around Exotica." Pearl took a deep breath. "One day, when aliens come to judge the human race, they are going to think we're full of shit."

Charlotte sat quietly, trying to absorb this new information. Slowly, her hands balled into fists, and she shouted, "Pearl, first of all, don't say the word s-h-i-t! You know I hate vulgar language. But even worse, I hate people who contribute to the destruction of this beautiful universe. We've already destroyed Earth. Our poor planet is dying. Now we're going to pollute outer space? That's a whole new level of destruction." She wrinkled her nose in disgust and sputtered, "Hopefully they'll run out of containers very soon. I don't even care what they're going to do after that."

"Well," Pearl smirked, "I guess they're just going to shoot their shit *au naturel*."

Completely ignoring her friend's crude remark, Charlotte said, "The thing I don't understand is why the families of these billion-aires don't hire their own team of specialists to come up with a solution. They could afford it."

"Guess what?" said Pearl. "Not a single one of the six families offered to contribute even a penny to get their family member back. It kind of makes me feel lucky. Money could never buy the kind of friendship that we have."

The three women sat deep in thought for a few moments, then threw their napkins over their half-eaten lunches and said, "I hope dessert is better than this meatloaf."

Aunt Clarice's Bloody-Good Pumpkin Pies

Clarice stood in front of her parents' dilapidated farmhouse, her eyes stinging with tears. Unemployed, single, and going broke, her self-esteem was in the toilet. If she couldn't come up with a way to earn some money quickly, she might lose the family farm. She shuddered as she thought about the upcoming mortgage payment and imagined her parents turning in their graves. With the pumpkin contest at the Wilcox County Fair coming up at the end of the summer, Clarice was desperate to win and vowed to do whatever it took.

Pumpkin growing was serious business in Wilcox County. The winner of the contest walked away with a check, a contract, and their photo on the front page of the *Wilcox Daily News*. Clarice knew that in the past, some of the winning pumpkins had weighed in at more than nine hundred pounds, so she had her work cut out for her.

The biggest draw for Clarice was that last year's winner, Savannah Abernathy, had been disqualified when it was discovered she'd watered her pumpkins with milk. Which meant this year, the prize money would be double. It would be almost enough to keep the farm afloat until the end of the year.

Clarice wandered around the farm in a daze, rolling her

problems around in her mind like marbles. When she reached the pumpkin patch, she dropped to her knees and began gently caressing the small leaves of her two-week-old seedlings. She used to help her parents sell pumpkins at the fair as a kid and was hoping to earn a few bucks by doing the same. As she began studying her plants, she noted they were bright, green, and healthy but not growing as quickly as she had hoped. She squeezed her head with her hands, willing her brain to come up with an idea to help them grow bigger.

With no ideas forthcoming, she dragged herself to the porch and plopped down on her father's ancient rocking chair. She began rocking back and forth aggressively as she pondered how she was pouring her blood, sweat, and tears into keeping this farm afloat—and just like that, inspiration rained down. She jumped into the air and shouted, "Yes!" She knew what she had to do. She would water her plants with blood. Not much, just a few drops a day. Heck, her diabetic friend Lucy shed more blood than that testing her sugar.

Clarice ran into the kitchen and plucked the rule book out of the junk drawer. After reading it from cover to cover, she learned there was absolutely nothing in the regulations against feeding the plants with blood, and she thought the heme might give the pumpkins a lovely, bright-orange color. The more she contemplated it, the better she liked the idea.

From that day on, Clarice pricked one of her fingers each morning and bled into the garden, rotating between areas. It was more painful than she'd imagined, and she had a renewed sense of sympathy for her friend Lucy.

Midway through the season, Clarice evaluated her garden, and it was clear not a single one of her pumpkins was on track to win the contest. With a heavy heart, she thought about discontinuing her bloodletting, but she had come so far that she decided to see it through.

A few days before the contest, Clarice's brother Clay and his twelve-year-old daughter Daria came to help her harvest the pumpkins. Clay was an accountant, and though he was happy to help Clarice at harvest time just like he had his parents, he had no desire to help her run the farm. He had moved to the big city, and he liked his life there.

The three family members worked together in the garden all afternoon, sweat dripping down their faces as they cut the pumpkins off the vines. When they finished, they dragged themselves into the kitchen, and Clarice poured out three large glasses of ice-cold lemonade.

After chugging down his drink, Clay looked at Clarice and said, "Hey, sis, do you think you can make a couple of pies for me and Daria to take home?" He smirked. "Of course, nobody can bake pies as delicious as Grandma Pearl's, but I have to admit, yours aren't too bad."

Clarice lightly punched her brother in the arm and nodded her head yes. She then sat down at the kitchen table, absently sipping her lemonade and losing herself in lovely memories of baking with her grandmother.

She could still picture her grandma's hands, like a magician's, rolling out the dough, gliding over the mixing bowls, and tossing in ingredients without ever using a recipe. Her pies smelled and tasted like heaven and were the highlight of every Thanksgiving dinner. As Grandma Pearl grew older and arthritis set in, she began teaching Clarice all her special techniques for baking the perfect pumpkin pie. The first time they baked together, Grandma Pearl whispered in Clarice's ear, "Now it's time to put in the special ingredient."

"What's that, Grandma?" asked Clarice with her eyes shining brightly.

"Why, it's love, my dear. Always bake your pies with love."

As she continued to float in her daydreams, an idea began to take shape. Clarice jumped up and shouted, "Hey, Clay, I know what I'll do! I'll make pumpkin pies for the fair. I never had time to do it before, but now that I'm unemployed, I can make loads of them. They'll bring in a lot more money than just selling pumpkins."

With a renewed sense of purpose, Clarice grabbed her car keys and purse, and the three of them slid into the car. When they got to the market, Clay pulled a wheelbarrow out of the trunk and they piled it high with all the ingredients they would need to bake a hundred pies. Clarice bubbled over with excitement at the idea of baking again and was pleased to be able to pass on the family tradition to Daria. She hoped the townsfolk would buy her pies in memory of her beloved grandmother, and that she would sell enough to be able to pay some of the bills.

On the day of the fair, Clarice arrived early and set up a booth between the corn-on-the-cob stand and the watermelon bins. She arranged her pies on the table and hung up the sign her niece had made: *Aunt Clarice's Pumpkin Pies.* Little did anyone know of Clarice's special ingredient.

Before she was even done setting up, a group of five young men walked by and began sniffing Clarice's pies like dogs. They looked to be in their late twenties, and they all had the same pasty-white complexion.

Clarice clenched her fists and shouted, "Excuse me, please stop sniffing my pies like that! It's very unsanitary."

She looked the boys over and recognized them as members of that strange new church in town, and suddenly her arm hairs stood on end. She couldn't put her finger on it, but there was something creepy about them. Even their church building was creepy. When she had driven past the week before, she noticed a sign on the front door that read C.O.L.D. The whole town was talking about how quickly the membership was growing, and people were becoming concerned.

Clarice gulped as she asked, "Can I help you?"

The oldest in the group stepped up and introduced himself as William. He furrowed his brows and questioned, "Hey, what do you put in your pies?" His mouth was watering, and saliva was beginning to drip down his chin.

Clarice responded, "It's a secret, but everyone loves my grandma's pies."

William rocked back on his heels, pulled out his wallet, and removed twenty-five dollars. He pressed the money into Clarice's hand, and when they touched, Clarice felt a mild electric current shoot through her. She took a moment to steady herself before holding out the pie.

William grabbed the sweet confection and immediately dug in his fist, shoving a handful into his mouth. Suddenly, he began spinning around in a frenzy, emitting an unnatural, guttural moan from deep within his throat.

Goose bumps prickled Clarice's skin as she watched William eat every last drop and lick the tin clean. He then nodded to his four friends, who each bought a pie and headed to the picnic area. Clarice grinned as she put one hundred and twenty-five dollars into her pocket.

Within a couple of hours, people from the church were pouring into the fair and heading directly for Clarice's pie stand. Before she knew it, she was completely sold out. She stood there counting her money over and over again in disbelief, relief flooding through her as she realized she could pay this month's mortgage. She put her hands together and looked up to the heavens in gratitude for the inspiration for her secret ingredient.

When Clay arrived to help her pack up, Clarice was deep in concentration. "What's up, sis?" he asked her.

She turned to him and sighed. "What would you think if I lived at the farm permanently and opened up a bakery? I've always loved baking, and I'm really good at it. I think this is what I'm meant to do."

Clay raised an eyebrow. "Are you crazy? Do you know how much money it costs to start a new business? You could never afford it." He shook his head. "Clarice, why don't you just cut your losses, sell the farm, and go back to working as a waitress? You know, maybe you could meet a guy and get married or something. That would be nice. Wouldn't it?"

That night, Clarice sat on her couch eating ice cream directly from the container and binge-watching episodes of *The Great British Baking Show* on Netflix. She knew her brother was right and was wallowing in self-pity.

Just as the tears began to flow, the doorbell rang. Clarice's heart started to thump as she wondered who the heck could be calling so late at night. Trembling, she got up and walked to the door. When she looked through the peephole and saw it was William from the weird church, her jaw dropped. She ran and grabbed her brother's baseball bat from the bedroom and opened the door a crack. She dried her tears and barked, "What are you doing here?"

William gave her a toothy smile and said, "Good evening, Clarice. I am here to present you will a business proposition. Do I have permission to come in?"

Clarice hesitated a few moments before opening the door all the way. When William stepped in, she gripped the bat tightly in her fists and motioned him to the couch. Despite being stunned by his sudden appearance, Clarice couldn't help being mesmerized by William's sparkling white teeth and dazzling smile. She made a mental note to ask him what teeth whitener he used if they ever became friends.

About an hour after his arrival, Clarice and William were shaking hands as business partners. Once again she felt the electric current, which was now mixed with her adrenaline, and her whole body was buzzing. Her dreams were coming true. She was going to have her very own bakery, named after her beloved grandmother. The church would put up all the money for Grandma Pearl's Bakery, get all the permits, and take care of the paperwork. Clarice's job while waiting would be to create and test new pastry recipes and plan her garden for the next spring. Members of the church would become her farm hands and help her grow pumpkins and blueberries and whatever else they decided on.

As Clarice escorted William to the door, she said, "I heard that C.O.L.D is short for Church of the Living Dead. Is that true?"

William winked at her and waved goodbye.

Clarice closed the door, grabbed a pen and paper, and sat back down on the couch. She googled how often a healthy person could donate blood and calculated from there. If she put two drops of her own blood in every pie, she could bake fifty pies a day and still maintain her health. If she hired some large assistants, she could triple or quadruple that number.

As she lay in bed that night unable to sleep, Clarice pictured William's face and smiled. He was really starting to grow on her. Sure, his complexion was a little pasty, he had the biggest teeth she had ever seen, and his table manners were appalling, but she just knew they could make beautiful pies together.

Message from the Other Side

Everyone tiptoed on eggshells around Gracie, especially her dad. You just never knew what to expect. One minute she might act like her normal, friendly self, and the next she would be picking nasty fights with her family and friends or just bursting into tears. Ever since her mother died ten months earlier, her behavior had become erratic.

That's why, when Gracie asked Mandy to accompany her to Mrs. Wilson's house to trick-or-treat, Mandy was too afraid to say no. Instead, she pleaded, "Do we have to, Gracie? I'm tired, and I still have homework. Please, can we just go home?" She took a step closer to Gracie and whispered into her ear. "Besides, my brother said that Mrs. Wilson's house is haunted. It's creeping me out."

Gracie stomped her foot and bellowed, "You're supposed to be my best friend, Mandy! Why can't we ever do what I want to do?" Tears sprang to her eyes, and she covered her face with her hands, ashamed of how mean she was behaving toward her friend. She stood for a few minutes without moving, took some deep breaths. Finally, she said, "I'm sorry, Mandy. I don't know what's wrong with me. Please come."

What she hadn't told Mandy was that she could swear she heard her mom's voice calling to her, beckoning her to Mrs. Wilson's house, and she was terrified to go alone. She couldn't tell if it was real or if she was imagining it, but she knew she had to go.

Mandy looked at her distraught friend, and a wave of sympathy washed over her. She held Gracie's hand and began swinging it like they used to when they were seven. She nodded her head. "Okay, I'll come with you."

As they turned toward Mrs. Wilson's house, Mandy thought about the conversation she'd had with her mother that morning. Sitting at the breakfast table, staring into her bowl of Cheerios, Mandy had whined, "Gracie's not fun anymore. She's always in a bad mood. I don't even know if I want to go trick-or-treating with her."

Mandy's mom sat next to her and put her arm around her shoulders. "Don't say that, honey. You and Gracie have been best friends since kindergarten. You've gone trick-or-treating together for seven years. Don't give up on her." She paused for a moment and pushed up her glasses. "Just think about how sad and angry Gracie must be feeling, and how much she suffered during her mom's long illness." She stroked her daughter's hair. "Gracie needs you now more than ever."

Mandy sighed deeply. "When is she going to be okay again, Mom?"

Her mother shrugged her shoulders and poured her another glass of milk. "It will take as long as it takes."

When they approached Mrs. Wilson's house, the girls stopped for a moment to assess it for creepiness. What they saw was a bright, well-kept house decorated with cheerful pumpkins, and though there seemed to be nothing unusual about it, it had a certain aura that made the girls feel uneasy.

Mandy stealthily pulled out her phone and texted her mother. *We're at creepy Mrs. Wilson's house. Call the police if you don't hear from me in five minutes.* She slipped the phone back into her pocket, and the girls clutched hands as they slowly trudged toward the door.

"We don't have to do this," mumbled Mandy. "We can still turn around and go home."

"No," replied Gracie. "I do have to do this." Gracie's hand began to tremble as she pressed the doorbell.

A minute later, a melodious voice rang out, "Who is it?"

Feeling anxious, the girls squeezed each other's hands as they sang out in unison, "Trick-or-treat."

Mrs. Wilson opened the door with a warm smile on her face and a bowl of candy in her hands. She looked at the girls and exclaimed, "Wonder Woman and Scarlet Witch! How cute are you?" She then winked at Gracie and said, "We've been expecting you. Come on in."

Gracie furrowed her brows, a bit taken aback that someone she hardly knew would invite her into their house. As she puffed up her chest to say absolutely not, she risked a quick peek into the living room. What she saw caused her to freeze like a block of ice. Her bag of candy dropped to the ground and spilled all over the porch. Her eyes flew open wide, and the color drained from her face. There, sitting on Mrs. Wilson's couch, was her mother, and she looked beautiful and healthy.

Gracie's mother's face lit up when she spotted her daughter, and she crooned, "Come on in, honey. It's okay. It's really me."

Gracie's heart began to race, and she clutched her head in disbelief, wondering if this was what it felt like to go crazy. She wanted it to be her mother so badly, but she couldn't understand what was happening. She took a few slow, tentative steps toward the couch, stopped, and then ran the rest of the way. She threw her arms around her mom only to discover they passed right through her, and she was hugging herself.

She blurted out, "Is this for real?"

Mrs. Wilson turned to her and smiled kindly. "I sometimes have special guests pay me a visit on Halloween Eve. Today, you and your mom are my VIP guests."

As reality set in, Gracie collapsed to the floor and began to sob. "I'm sorry, Mommy, I'm sorry, I'm sorry, I'm sorry!"

Her voice escalated with pain until her mom yelled, "Gracie Lynn Spencer, stop it right now!" Gracie snapped to attention as she always had when her mom called her by her full name and sat poised to listen. Her mother looked her in the eye and said, "There is nothing for you to feel sorry about."

Gracie's breath was coming in gulps, and she rasped, "But I wasn't at the hospital when you died. I went to Sophie's birthday party instead. I knew how sick you were, but I went to the party anyway. I never said goodbye. You must hate me. I hate me. I will never be happy again."

"No," her mother snapped, giving her a stern look. "I could never hate you. Not in a million years. You have nothing to be sorry about. You're just a kid who wanted to go to a party. You just wanted to feel normal for a change. You didn't make the decision on your own. Your father and I wanted you to get a break." She took a ghostly breath. "That's why Dad drove you there."

She looked down and dabbed at her eyes. "You didn't know it would be my last day. Nobody did. When I passed, I felt your love swirling around me. I know you loved me, and I love you to heaven and back. So," she huffed, "you need to get rid of that guilt that's weighing you down and begin to process your grief. It's okay to be sad and to miss me, but don't you dare feel guilty. Got it?"

The tears continued to pour down Gracie's face as she choked out, "I got it."

Gracie's mother smiled sadly. "I have to go now, sweetheart, but I couldn't leave this world without giving you this message." She turned to Mrs. Wilson. "Thanks for inviting us today. Now I can move on in peace." She blew Gracie a kiss and said, "Goodbye, sweetheart. Have fun, be happy, and tell your brother and Daddy I will watch over you always."

Gracie sat on the couch and sniffled, "Bye, Mommy. I'll never forget you."

For the next few minutes, Gracie sat in stunned silence as she watched her mother's image slowly disappear. When it was all over, she felt the weight of her guilt begin to lift off her shoulders and float away. She was free. Gracie continued to sit on the couch, deep in thought, until suddenly she turned to Mrs. Wilson and gasped, "Oh, my God, I left Mandy standing outside by herself! I've been in here for like an hour. She must be so worried."

Gracie raced outside just in time to see Mandy bending down to pick up her candy. Gracie joined her on the ground. "I'm so sorry for taking so long. You must have been so scared when I went into the house."

Mandy wrinkled her nose. "What are you talking about? We just got here. I don't know what happened that you suddenly dropped your bag of candy, but let's just pick it up and go home."

When they finished cleaning up, Mrs. Wilson gave them each two full-sized Hershey bars and waved goodbye.

As they skipped to the end of the walkway, Mandy pulled out her phone to text her mother that they were leaving Mrs. Wilson's. She noticed they had only been there for three minutes. She remarked to her friend, "Mrs. Wilson is really nice. I don't know why my brother said her house is haunted. He's so dumb."

"Yeah," said Gracie. "I really like her. You know, before my mom got sick, she used to say we should have tea with Mrs. Wilson. My mom was worried she was lonely." Gracie looked down at the ground. "But we never got the chance." She kicked an empty soda can on the sidewalk and suddenly perked up. "Hey, I know!

I'll visit her next weekend. Maybe I'll bring some muffins."

Mandy shrugged her shoulders. "That's nice of you. Maybe I'll join you. By the way," she added, "my mom is making fried chicken tonight. Wanna have dinner at my house? Afterward, we can trade candy."

"Yeah," said Gracie. "I think I'd like that. Let me just call my dad." And as she took her phone out of her pocket, she truly smiled for the first time in a very long time.

Angela's Super-Surprise Wedding

Angela zipped up her plus-sized wedding dress and cringed as she looked in the mirror. This was not how she had imagined her wedding day would be. She sat down on her bed, closed her eyes, and recalled the dreams she'd had as a young girl. Those dreams were as vivid now as they had ever been. Dreams of walking down the aisle on her father's arm in a beautiful lace gown. Her friends oohing and aahing at how beautiful she looked. Her tall, handsome groom waiting for her at the altar, tears streaming down his face.

She basked in her wonderful memories, a smile lighting her face, until the whistling of the tea kettle jolted her back to reality. The truth was that her father had passed away ten years earlier, and now her mother was gone as well. The perfect wedding was no longer in the cards for her.

At fifty-two, Angela had the beginnings of a turkey neck, was tired-looking, and was fifty pounds overweight; she reckoned the fat on her stomach alone could double as the flower girl. Despite her misgivings, she got up and went to the bathroom to put on some makeup. She was determined to make this day, her wedding day, as wonderful as it could be.

As she began applying her lipstick, Angela thought, for the

thousandth time, about the day just two weeks earlier when this web of deceit had begun.

The day had started out just like any ordinary day. Angela's alarm went off at six in the morning, and she trudged into the kitchen and popped a pod into the Keurig. As she opened the refrigerator door to take out the milk, her phone began to buzz. She jumped a foot into the air, startled that somebody would call so early in the morning. When she looked down and saw that it was Debbie calling, her heart skipped a beat. Her best friend would never call that early unless something was terribly wrong.

She answered the phone in a panic. "Debbie, what's the matter? Please tell me you're okay."

Debbie sighed. "I'm fine, and I'm so sorry to call you this early in the morning, but I have a favor to ask, and I have to do it right now before I lose my nerve. Please hear me out before you say anything."

"You're starting to scare me," Angela said. "You know I'm always here for you, whatever it is. We've been best friends for thirty years. I'd do anything for you."

"Anything? Well, do you remember my brother Benjamin?"

"Of course I remember Ben. I've met him a bunch of times. I like him, I think he's very nice."

"Yes, he is very, very nice." Debbie took in a sharp breath and hesitated before continuing. "Listen, Angela," she whispered, "something bad has happened. Ever since the pandemic, the company Ben works for has been in trouble, and now his hours have been cut so low he lost his health insurance. With all the alimony and child support payments he's had to make over the years, he was never able to save any money. Right now, he can barely afford his rent, much less insurance premiums."

Debbie sniffled as she continued. "Here's the really scary part.

Ben has diabetes and high blood pressure, and he can't afford his medicine anymore. He's been breaking his pills in quarters and skipping his regular doctor visits. For God's sake, he's fifty-five and at the mercy of a healthcare system that doesn't care what happens to him. He's too poor to buy insurance, but he still earns too much money to qualify for Medicaid. You know, my mother had diabetes too, and she ended up having both her legs amputated."

"Yes, I know," Angela said. "I remember how depressed your mom became when she had to go into a wheelchair. It was awful."

Debbie began to cry. "Yes, it was the beginning of the end, and I don't want that to happen to Ben. I'm so scared for him. If there was just some way we could help him."

"I'm so sorry," Angela said. "What can I do to help? Does he need a loan?"

Debbie continued to cry. "No, he doesn't need a loan. He needs a wife. A wife with health insurance." Her sobs intensified and she choked out, "I'm asking you to marry him. Your nursing job gives you great health insurance, and if you were married, he'd be covered too. Please help him, Angela. Please, save his life."

Angela's eyes flew open at that stunning request, and she yelled into the phone, "Debbie, are you crazy? That's against the law! Besides, no offense, but your brother kind of looks like Doc Brown from that time travel movie. He also grunts when he eats, and I've seen him pick his nose on more than one occasion."

Debbie hiccupped. "Oh, Angela, he's the only family I have left. Please help him. It could be good for you, too. You're always telling me how lonely you've become since your mother died. My brother is a good guy, and he's handy around the house. He could fix that leaky faucet in your kitchen. Plus, he has the same sense of humor as I do, and you love my jokes. Just imagine it's me moving in with you, only with unruly white hair and poor fashion sense.

By the way," she huffed, "I think Doc Brown is kind of attractive, and I'm pretty sure all men pick their noses."

After the call ended, a very dazed and confused Angela began frantically pacing the living room floor. She had told Debbie she would think about it, and though she had a lot of sympathy for her best friend, she couldn't understand how Debbie could ask a favor like that.

The more Angela thought about it, the more upset she became. Debbie knew how much she hated doing anything illegal. She would never even share her Netflix account, even when everyone else was doing it. She had always been the good girl, the one who did the right thing, the one who took care of both her parents, sacrificing her own happiness to stay by their sides. Not like her older sister who abandoned both her and her parents to get married and start her own family.

Angela went into the kitchen and began eating Mallomars, stuffing them into her mouth so quickly she could barely taste them. She hated herself for being a stress eater and hated the way she looked. After the eighth cookie, she felt a bit calmer and decided to call her sister for advice.

When her sister picked up, Angela said, "Hey, Janie, I have something important to ask you."

Janie blew out a breath. "Okay, but make it quick. I have to go to work."

Angela frowned; her sister rarely had time for her. Debbie was a better sister to her than her own sister. "Okay, here it is. I'm contemplating getting married. What do you think?"

Janie's mouth dropped open, and her phone fell to the floor. Angela winced as the thud echoed in her ear. "Getting married? To whom?"

"Well, to Benjamin. You remember Ben, my friend Debbie's

brother. We've been spending a lot of time together and are think-ing of tying the knot."

Debbie barked into the phone, "Don't do it, Angela! Haven't you read any of the stories about older single women being scammed by con artists? These men marry desperate women and then take half their assets. You own the house. Can't you see he wants half the house and half your money? Besides, I think I've met Ben. Isn't he that guy with the wild hair that looks a bit like Doc Brown?"

Angela felt all the blood rush to her head as she rasped to her sister, "Are you saying the only reason a man would marry me is for my money? That's a horrible thing to say. And by the way, there are a lot of women who think Doc Brown is attractive."

"Oh, Angela, calm down," snorted Janie. "You know I'm only trying to help you. I'm not saying you're not lovable. I love you, and my kids love you too. You're their favorite aunt. Now don't take this the wrong way, but we have to face facts. You've let your-self go. I just don't want you to do anything stupid."

Angela hung up the phone without saying goodbye and stormed into her mother's room. She wished she still had a landline so that she could have slammed down the receiver in her sister's ear. In a fit of rage, she picked up a framed photo of herself and Janie as little girls and smashed it on the floor. The glass shattered into thousands of tiny shards and scattered under the bed. With her heart still pounding, Angela opened the top dresser drawer and took out her mom's jewelry box.

After staring at the box for a few minutes, Angela pulled out a small delicate pouch and gently opened it. Inside was the engage-ment ring her mother had left to her, the one she never wore be-cause as a single woman, she was too embarrassed to put it on. Angela poured the ring into her hand and placed it on her fourth finger. She turned on all the lights and opened up the shades to get a good look.

What she saw took her breath away. The sunlight reflected brilliantly off the diamond, and a million tiny lights danced across the bedroom walls. Angela moved her hand from side to side, mesmerized by the shimmering jewel, and felt something shift inside her. The ring felt so good on her finger, and she had waited so long to wear it.

Angela thought about how for the past twenty-two years, she had made the same New Year's resolution. She was ready for it to come true. Angela said a quick prayer, took a deep breath, picked up her phone, and called Debbie.

"Okay, I'll do it," she gushed. "I'll marry Ben."

Two weeks later, Debbie and Ben picked Angela up at her house, and the three of them drove to city hall. Although Angela was well aware the marriage was a sham, she treated herself to a new, white dress and had her hair professionally colored and cut.

When they arrived at the venue, Ben helped Angela off with her coat and smiled warmly at her. "Angela," he said, "you look lovely."

Angela's face turned crimson, and she sucked in a grateful breath that she'd shimmied into her Spanx that morning. As she regained her equanimity, Ben nodded to her, took her hand, and the couple walked in front of the judge.

As they said their I-dos, Angela shyly gazed upon Ben's face and wondered why she had never before noticed what beautiful brown eyes he had, and such a lovely smile. She also noticed he was wearing his best suit and had tamed his crazy hair, and she was touched he'd made the effort.

When the judge pronounced them man and wife, Ben gave her a small peck on the mouth. Angela blushed and ran her fingers over her lips. She hadn't been kissed in a very long time. The wedding had gone off without a hitch, and Debbie took about a thousand photos of the newlywed couple.

After leaving the courthouse, the threesome went to a Chinese restaurant to celebrate the fraudulent occasion and ordered the lunch special. The first course was wonton soup, and Angela gritted her teeth as Ben exuberantly slurped his soup. He was sucking it in so forcefully she was afraid he would swallow the whole spoon. Debbie kicked her brother under the table, and Angela made a mental note to never serve soup in the house. Once again, she wondered if she was crazy for doing this.

After the meal, Ben rented a van and brought his belongings to his new home. As he carried them in, Angela began directing him to her mother's room, but then she gritted her teeth and decided it was about time she took the master bedroom. He could have her much smaller bedroom.

That night, while Ben settled in, Angela cooked a nice dinner for the first time in over a year. Since her mother's passing, she had no oomph to cook for just herself. Every night it was either a frozen dinner or a meal picked up on the way home from work.

Angela stood in front of the oven and took a deep breath. The aroma of the roasting chicken and potatoes made her feel warm all over, and for just a moment, she forgot all about the strangeness of the current situation and delighted in having company for dinner.

When the chicken was ready, Angela arranged it on her mother's special occasion serving dish and called Ben to the table. As they ate their first dinner together, things were a bit uncomfortable. It was a strain to keep the conversation going, and there were a bunch of awkward silences. Afterward, Ben patted his stomach and said, "Angela, that was delicious. I'll do the dishes, and later maybe we could meet in the living room and watch a movie together. You know, get to know each other a bit more."

Angela felt tears pricking her eyes. Nobody had washed the dishes for her or appreciated her cooking in a very, very long time. Her voice cracked as she said, "Thank you, Ben. I'd like that."

After Ben finished up in the kitchen, he walked into the living room and saw that Angela had spread out all her favorite DVDs on the floor. "How about *Love Actually*?" she asked.

Ben said, "Nah, I don't like romantic comedies. How about we stream the new Batman movie?"

"Nah," said Angela. "I hate superhero movies."

They went back and forth a few more times before they both said in unison, "How about a sci-fi movie?"

Finally, something Angela and Ben could agree on. Angela went into the kitchen and microwaved some popcorn as Ben popped *Back to the Future* into the DVD player. She returned to the living room carrying a large bowl of aromatic popcorn and sat next to Ben on the couch. As the newlyweds watched the movie together, they grew more comfortable with each laugh they shared.

When the movie was over, it was already late, and both Angela and Ben had to get up early for work the next day. On the way to his new bedroom, Ben turned and said, "Good night, Angela, and thank you for everything. Your name suits you. You really are an angel."

Angela closed her bedroom door feeling giddy. Among all the weirdness of the day, there was a lot to be excited about. It was wonderful having a husband.

She impulsively reached for her laptop, glanced at the ring on her finger, and launched the Facebook app. Then, with a brilliant smile spreading across her face, she changed her status to married. Immediately, her phone began to buzz, and she saw that it was

Janie. She climbed into bed and turned off her phone. Her sister could wait until morning.

The Cake That Melted Sorrows

It was almost the first Friday of the month—or as the ladies in the medical billing office liked to call it, "Ditch the Diet Friday." Once a month, a group of women in the workplace got together for a festive luncheon of takeout fried chicken, fried potatoes, and a homemade decadent dessert. And each month, Sara's face burned with shame as she turned down yet another invitation. After a while, inviting Sara to the luncheon became an office joke, so on the day that she said yes, everybody's mouth dropped open.

For a full minute, Sara's coworkers stared at her in stunned silence, until Molly exclaimed, "Wow, Sara, great!" A grin spread across her face as she added, "First-timers bring dessert."

The moment Sara said yes, she could feel her heart begin to race. She had been in therapy for social anxiety for a while now, and her therapist said she was ready for the next step. She didn't feel ready, but at twenty-six years old and having never been on a date, she was desperate to try anything.

With sweat beading on her forehead, Sara pushed back her chair and began doing her deep-breathing exercises, but instead of calming her, it was causing her to hyperventilate. She could feel herself spiraling into a full panic attack and knew the only thing that would help was her anti-anxiety medicine. Sara craned her neck to make sure nobody was watching, opened up the little plastic bag she kept in her top desk drawer, and gulped down a Xanax.

She passed the remainder of the afternoon distracted, debating whether she should call in sick the next day, and by the time she left the office, she was completely overwhelmed. She walked to her bus stop worrying about the luncheon and spent the entire bus ride home googling cake recipes as she peeled off all her nail polish.

Flecks of pink piled up on her skirt as she scrolled through dozens of websites, agonizing over which recipe to choose. With time running out, she decided on a red velvet cake with chocolate cream frosting, topped with maraschino cherries. She really hoped nobody was allergic to chocolate.

When she got off the bus, Sara went directly to the market and carefully picked out all the ingredients she would need for the cake. Though it was dinner time when she walked through her door, she had no appetite and decided to get right to work.

She opened her cabinets and banged around until she found just the right pans for a double-layer cake. Baking was the kind of solitary activity that Sara regularly enjoyed, and she had all the right equipment. She was the official birthday cake maker of the family, and her grandmother always said her cakes were a work of art. She had many hours of watching *Cupcake Wars* to thank for that.

After placing the mixing bowls and measuring spoons on the kitchen counter, Sara preheated the oven and turned on some music to help her relax. Carefully, she measured out all the ingredients and poured them into the bowl, blending them together until she had a rich, thick, aromatic batter.

As she got ready to pour the batter into the pan, suddenly, angry butterflies of dread began fluttering around her stomach, and she started obsessing over how everyone in her office must think she was such a loser.

Her adrenaline began to soar, and she groaned, "Oh, no, not again," and reached for her bottle of pills.

Sara's hands shook as she struggled to pull off the child-proof cap, and when it finally opened, one of her pills popped out and dropped into the batter. She quickly removed it with a spoon and began to berate herself for being clumsy, but then an interesting thought crossed her mind. She stopped what she was doing and rubbed her chin.

Hmmm, she thought, smiling for the first time that day. Yes, it was a brilliant idea. She grabbed five more pills, ground them up, and poured them into the batter. She figured if she put Xanax in the cake, she could take her medication without anybody knowing her secret shame. She felt a tad guilty, but it was a tiny dose, and she knew the half-life of the medication was very short, so her coworkers would be back to normal before quitting time.

Sara arrived at work early the next morning and placed her cake in the refrigerator. The cake had turned out perfectly, and she knew that even if people didn't enjoy her company, they would at least appreciate the cake.

At 12:01, she trudged into the lunchroom on leaden feet and was immediately hit by the most heavenly smells of fried chicken and potatoes. Having skipped breakfast, her stomach growled ferociously, and she stood at the door, watching her coworkers setting up and chatting animatedly.

Camille was putting on festive tablecloths, Molly was paying the delivery guy for the chicken, Joanie was taking out the beverages, Nicole was reaching for the paper plates, and Jess was putting up decorations. The drab office lunchroom was transforming into a party, and the air was abuzz with excitement.

Sara couldn't help smiling as she took her cake out of the refrigerator and expertly arranged it on a platter with a maraschino cherry garnish. When she placed the dessert on the table, there were oohs and aahs all around and she blushed, feeling thankful that relief from her nervousness was just one slice away.

She took a seat at the table just as Molly was picking up the bucket of chicken to pass around. As she handed it to Camille, Sara whispered, "Umm, if it's okay with you guys, I think I'm going to start with a piece of cake."

Sara's five coworkers stared at her blankly until Molly blurted out, "Sara, that's an inspired idea! Cut me a slice as well."

Before she knew it, Sara found herself slicing the cake into six portions, and the women were laughing like schoolgirls as they accepted their guilty pleasure.

As the group began digging into their cake, Camille closed her eyes and moaned. "Mmmm, Sara, why didn't you ever tell us about your hidden talent?"

You could hear a pin drop as the six coworkers ate their cake slowly, savoring every delectable drop. When they finished, they began peppering Sara with questions about her recipe and baking techniques, her favorite things to talk about. By the time the chicken was passed around, the Xanax had begun to work its magic, and Sara was having a good time.

As the women chatted away, Sara listened to Camille complain about how hard it was to raise a son with a disability. Molly groaned about how her hot flashes were going to be her undoing. Joanie cried over her recent breakup, and Sara learned that every single one of her coworkers had big problems and worries just like her. She suddenly felt brave enough to talk about her social anxiety, and everybody was kind and sympathetic.

By the end of the luncheon, all six of the women were relaxed and smiling, and Camille even commented that she felt as if a load had been lifted off her shoulders. As they got ready to head back to the office, Sara's five coworkers took a vote and unanimously decided that it was Sara's job from then on to bring the dessert.

They made her promise to always attend their monthly luncheons, and Sara nodded her head yes as a giant lump formed in her throat.

The second time Sara baked the cake for "Ditch the Diet Fry-day," she put Xanax in it for reassurance, but by her third Fry-day, Sara had begun to feel better about socializing and didn't need the medicine as much anymore. Little by little, she was becoming good friends with Nicole and Jess from the office, and they helped her feel confident enough to register on a dating website.

Between her therapy and her new friends at the office, Sara was branching out and beginning to feel comfortable in her own skin. With her popularity and her self-esteem rising, the only special ingredients Sara now added to her cakes were love, gratitude, and a little extra chocolate.

Fresh Meat

Tania had been stranded on the desert island for two long years, with nothing to eat but coconuts, when she spotted a man stepping off a boat. She ran to him sobbing, jumped into his arms, and clocked him over the head with a rock.

"Yes!" she cried. "Fresh meat!"

The Girl on the Bridge

"Hey, what's in the package?" Julie asked as her mother brought in the mail.

"I don't know," Violet replied. "I wasn't expecting anything."

She strolled into the kitchen and pulled a pair of scissors from the junk drawer, grinning with anticipation as she cut through the many layers of adhesive tape. When the package was finally open, she pulled out a book and frowned.

"What's this? I didn't order a book. I hope this isn't some sort of scam."

Julie skipped over to take a look. "Oh, Mom," she gushed, "that's Olivia Green's latest book. *The Girl on the Bridge* is on my summer reading list. I heard it's fantastic. Pass it over." She grabbed the book out of her mother's hands and rifled through the first few pages. When she read the dedication, she gasped. "Mom, look! Olivia dedicated the book to you! She wrote, 'For Violet Adams, my hero.' Mom, what did you do?"

Violet took the book back from her daughter and stared at the dedication page. She scratched her head as she mumbled, "Olivia…Olivia…Olivia." Suddenly, her eyes lit up. "Of course! Olivia was the girl on the bridge all those years ago!" She sat on the couch and hugged the book to her chest. "I always wondered what happened to her. I'm so happy to see she's done well."

Julie stood in front of her mother and crossed her arms. "Don't just sit there, Mom. Tell me what happened."

Violet shook her head. "It's really not a big deal. Around twenty years ago, I was on the way to a blind date when I noticed a teenager sitting on the Manhattan Bay Bridge sobbing. I had a bad feeling about it, so I got out of the car to see if she was okay. I ended up driving her to Drink-n-Donuts, and we spent two hours chatting over coffee and chocolate chip muffins."

Julie's eyes opened wide. "You spent two hours talking to Olivia Green? That's so cool!"

Violet grinned, happy to be considered cool by her daughter for any reason. "To make a long story short, once we got our food, Olivia's problems came pouring out like hot lava. She told me about how she was being bullied at school and how lonely she felt. At first, I wasn't sure what to do. I mean, I'm not a psychologist or anything, so I just told her about how I'd been depressed in high school too." She looked down at the floor. "I knew exactly how she felt. Anyway, I promised her it would get better and gave her my phone number in case she wanted to talk. She never called."

"Holy crap, Mom," Julie exclaimed. "Olivia's new book is about teen suicide. I think you might have saved her life. You're like a real hero."

"Hero, shmero," laughed Violet. "All I did that day was buy a girl a cup of coffee."

A Matter of Respect

The soft glow of candlelight combined with the salty smell of the ocean confirmed for Sara and Charlie that El Pescado Dorado was the perfect choice for an anniversary dinner. The upscale restaurant had been on the bucket list of the lifelong foodies, and they had starved themselves all day in anticipation of an outstanding meal.

Upon being seated, Sara reached across the table and placed her shaky hand into her husband's, knowing his gentle touch would help her calm down. It had been a bumpy journey to their table, and though Charlie was an excellent driver, it was never easy to maneuver her wheelchair across a crowded room. Sara closed her eyes and wondered if she would ever get used to people staring at her.

Charlie squeezed his wife's hand in sympathy, and Sara began to feel better, pondering how lucky she was to have such a thoughtful husband. In anticipation of a navigational disaster, he had called the restaurant ahead of time and asked that they have a bottle of wine waiting for them at the table. The maître d' poured two glasses right away.

When they were alone, Sara picked up her glass to propose a toast but quickly put it down when she noticed her husband was sulking. Charlie had bumped her into a few chairs on the way in, and she could see he was feeling guilty. Sara took a breath, looked him in the eye and smirked. "It's okay, Charlie. If you feel that bad, you can give me your dessert."

Charlie frowned in mock anger. "No, no. I'm feeling much better now."

With his spirits restored, Sara again raised her glass and made a toast to ten wonderful years. She clinked her glass with Charlie's and polished off two drinks in quick succession. She wasn't a big drinker and knew two glasses were all it would take to help her relax.

As she began to loosen up, Sara picked up her menu and studied the descriptions of the dinner items with the precision of a scientist. Though she and Charlie dined out often, restaurants like El Pescado Dorado were a once-a-year splurge, and she was determined to order the perfect dish.

She peeked over her menu and stealthily glanced around the dining area, taking note of what everyone else was eating. The young couple at the next table were enjoying broiled lobster, cracking the shells and dipping the meat into the freshly drawn butter. Sara's mouth began to water as she swiveled her chair to look in the other direction. On her left, a gentleman was cutting into a medium-rare steak the size of Texas as his companion greedily sucked the meat out from an oversized king crab leg.

Hmmm, she thought. *That looks yummy too.*

Sara turned to Charlie, and they began a lengthy discussion about what to order, debating the pros and cons of each dish. When a decision was finally made, Charlie got the waiter's attention and waved him over. As the server began heading in their direction, Sara smiled, admiring his freshly pressed black tuxedo and polished leather shoes.

When the young man approached, he locked eyes on Sara's chair and momentarily froze. Quickly averting his gaze, he turned to Charlie and asked, "Are you ready to order, sir? What can I get you?"

Charlie said, "I'll have the surf and turf with a baked potato and creamed spinach, and we'll have another bottle of wine, please." He closed his menu and handed it to the waiter, expecting he would now turn around and face Sara.

What happened instead was that he continued to look at Charlie and asked, "And what will the lady be having?"

It wasn't the first time Sara had been treated as less-than because of her wheelchair, and her usual response was to clear her throat and bark, "Excuse me, I'm over here!" But this evening, fueled by too much alcohol and two years of built-up rage since the accident, she decided to take matters into her own hands. Sara calmly removed the straw from her water glass, made a spitball out of a piece of napkin, and blew it at the waiter's head.

The young man's hand shot to the back of his head, and he began to rub it. He had no clue what had just happened and stood there with a puzzled look on his face. He turned back to Charlie, who was now grinning. "I'm sorry, sir, what will the lady be having?"

Sara formed another spitball, and this time blew it at the back of the young man's head with every ounce of her breath.

The waiter yipped, rubbed his head, and turned to look at Sara, who was waving the straw in his face and scowling. As the realization of his rudeness sank in, the waiter's face turned a deep crimson. He bowed to Sara and said, "I am truly sorry, madam. It won't happen again. What can I get you?"

Sara said, "I'll have the grilled salmon with apricot sauce and a baked potato with sour cream and chives." She winked at the waiter. "Oh, and we'll have a complimentary slice of double chocolate layer cake for dessert. Don't forget the whipped cream."

The waiter stuttered, "Of course, madam" and walked away with his head down.

Not in Anybody's Shadow: Memoirs of Dick Grayson (AKA Robin, AKA The Boy Wonder)

Chapter One: Nobody's Shadow

Let me set the record straight. I have never dwelled in anybody's shadow, especially not Batman's. In all my years as a superhero, I have always been my own person. I did not become Batman's sidekick because I was insecure or had some sort of deficit. I was his sidekick because I chose to be.

You see, Bruce Wayne saved my life, and though he never asked for any compensation, I wanted to do something for him. After I witnessed the brutal death of my parents as a kid, I became an orphan, full of rage with PTSD. Batman took me in when nobody else would. He became my family, gave me a place to live, an identity—and believe me, it wasn't too shabby living in a mansion with a billionaire. I had a lot of cool gadgets and a sweet car.

Most people don't know this, but my role as Batman's sidekick was twofold: fighting crime and making sure Bruce was not swallowed up by the darkness that threatened to consume him. As his adopted son and one half of the dynamic duo, I was the only person that could keep him from committing atrocities. His voice of reason, if you will. I can't tell you how many times I asked him to see a therapist, but the stubborn jackass just wouldn't do it. But I did. I worked out my issues. I became not just a crime fighter, but a husband and a father, and I lived a very fulfilling life.

That's why when I read the poem written about me by that hack of a writer named Peggy Gerber, I just knew I had to respond. This is what she wrote:

Holly Cannoli Batman, it's my Time to Shine
Always the sidekick,
Never the hero

Robin dwelled in
Batman's shadow

Knowing he would always
Be second best

Stuck in the passenger seat, never
taking the wheel of his own life

Nobody wants to be Robin
for Halloween

First of all, Ms. Gerber, I haven't said "holy cannoli" since the nineteen sixties. Do your research. Second of all, when I took my grandsons trick-or-treating this October, I counted five different people dressed up as me for Halloween. Granted, it was the dads wearing my outfit while their sons were dressed as Batman, but one could argue that Robin was the much more important role. Those Batmans would be nothing without their Robins. Some of the Batmans weren't even old enough to cross the street by themselves.

Thus, Ms. Gerber, if you think I never took the wheel of my own life, you are completely wrong. In fact, I am more beloved and more famous than you'll ever be. At eighty years old, paparazzi still wait by my front door each morning.

So, Ms. Gerber, if I haven't made it clear, your poem stinks, but I do thank you for inciting me to write this memoir.

Chapter Two: The Beginning

Voodoo Bullseye

anine was sprawled on the couch binge-eating chocolate chip cookies when she heard a knock at the door.

"Go away!" she shouted as she pulled the blanket over her head. "I told you, I'm not celebrating my birthday this year."

"Open the door," yelled Maggie. "If you don't, we're going to sing 'Happy Birthday' right here in your hallway."

Quicker than Janine could even stash the cookies under her couch pillow, her two best friends began raucously singing at the top of their lungs, as if they were drunk. Janine raced to the door, flung it open, and pulled her friends in by their collars.

"Maggie," Janine grumbled, "I told you I just wanted to be by myself."

Erin shook her head. "No, Janine, you're coming with us. Remember what your therapist said? It's okay to be sad about your divorce, but it's not okay to stop your life. So take your expensive therapist's advice and get ready. We're going out."

Janine knew her friends well enough to grasp they wouldn't take no for an answer, so she huffed off to her room to get dressed. Moving at the speed of a turtle, she put on her ratty yoga pants and her ancient Mickey Mouse sweatshirt. It was her way of saying "You can take me out, but you can't force me to have a good time." She clenched her fists in frustration. How could her friends think she could enjoy herself when in just a few days she would be signing her divorce papers?

When Janine emerged from her room, Erin's eyes opened as wide as saucers. She sneered. "Oh, my God, why did you put on a clown suit? We're not going to the circus. Please go change."

Janine glared at Erin with such ferocity that she felt her eyeballs beginning to melt. Eric put her head down and stammered, "What I meant to say is that Maggie and I are so happy you decided to join us."

Janine, feeling a tad guilty for upsetting her friends, put on her coat quickly. "So where are we actually going? Not that it makes a difference, but there better not be birthday cake."

A grin lit up Maggie's face. "We're going to that new ax-throwing place called Karmaax. You know, the one that just opened up on Route 666. It's got fantastic reviews."

Janine shook her head and snorted. "Ax throwing! Is that even a real thing? And what kind of name is Karmaax. It sounds like we'll be chopping down trees in an auto repair shop. I don't think so. Let's just get a drink."

"No," exclaimed Erin, "we already reserved the room for an hour, and it's non-refundable. Besides, I think you're going to like our little surprise."

Janine trudged to the car two feet behind her friends and climbed into the backseat, thinking about how this was shaping up to be the worst birthday of her life. "This is stupid. I've never thrown an ax in my life. I'm not even good at darts."

Erin sighed. "Come on, Janine. Maggie and I worked really hard to plan this event for you. Try to keep an open mind."

After a tense car ride, the women walked into Karmaax, and a leather-clad woman named Zenobia escorted them to their reserved room. As they entered, Zenobia pointed to the wall, and Janine immediately spotted her surprise. Her face lit up, and she threw back her head and laughed. Her friends had emailed a photo of her soon-to-be ex-husband, and the staff had turned it into a special target just for her.

"I hope you like it," said Zenobia. "Custom-made targets are our specialty." She looked directly at Janine and winked. "Just think of it as a voodoo doll." She then gave the women a tutorial on how to throw axes and asked them to leave a positive Google review.

After she left, Janine gasped, "Holy cow, the owner of this place is super creepy. I've never seen so many tattoos on one person before. But," she added with a grin, "this might actually be fun." She rubbed her hands together and announced, "I'll go first."

As Janine stared at the target, a sneer began to cross her face. She took a deep breath, pulled back her arms, and threw the ax with such force it bounced right off the target. Each time her turn came around, she grabbed the ax and threw it fast and furiously without any kind of aim, alleviating herself of months of built-up rage.

Along with each of her throws came a bark of fury. "Take that, you stupid jerk, for cheating on me! Take that, you selfish moron, for betraying my trust! Take that, you son of a bitch, for not fighting for me!"

At 9:59 p.m., as their hour was coming to an end, a very exhausted Janine prepared for her final throw. She knit her brows in deep concentration, pulled her arms behind her head, and took aim.

"Bullseye!" she bellowed when the ax landed between her husband's eyes. She pumped her fists into the air and shouted, "Yes!"

Impressed by Janine's success, her friends applauded enthusiastically. She took a bow.

"Thanks, girls," Janine said. "I really needed this. I feel like a wrecking ball has been lifted from my shoulders." She looked at her friends and added, "I'm ready to celebrate my birthday. Let's go have a drink."

After what turned out to be a surprisingly fun-filled evening, a slightly inebriated Janine got out of Maggie's car feeling lighter than she had in a long time. Her friends shouted through the windows, "You're going to be okay, Janine. Just stay strong."

Janine walked into her apartment smiling and threw her keys on the kitchen table. She began belting out "I Will Survive" as she poured herself a glass of water. Still humming, she walked into her bedroom and took her phone out of her purse. When she saw she had a missed call from her mother-in-law, she became stone-cold sober and she hissed under her breath, "What does the Wicked Witch of the West want now?"

With shaky hands, she opened her voicemail and pressed play. As she listened to the message, her eyes flew open and the phone dropped to the floor.

"Oh, my God!" she shrieked as she stared at the phone in disbelief. Her heart now pounding, she picked up the phone and listened to the message three more times in an effort to process it.

At approximately 10:00 p.m., her husband had collapsed in his girlfriend's apartment and was brought to the hospital by ambulance. He had suffered a grand mal seizure and was being admitted. The doctors were recommending he stay in the hospital for a couple of days for tests and observation. Meanwhile, since the divorce was not yet final and her husband was still groggy, her mother-in-law demanded she come to the hospital right away.

Janine slumped onto the couch and put her hands over her head. As she sat pondering what had happened, a horrible thought crossed her mind. Was this her fault?

Slowly, she moved her hands in front of her eyes and examined them closely. These were the hands that had thrown the ax at her husband's face. A sudden chill whipped through her, and she decided to take a hot shower to warm up.

As the streaming water pelted her shoulders, she began repeating the name of the establishment in her head. *Karmaax…Karmaax…Karma ax.*

"Oh, my God," she gasped. "Is this some sort of mystical karma? I knew there was something weird about that place."

With guilt beginning to swirl through her, Janine picked up the phone to order an Uber when she suddenly remembered her husband had collapsed inside his girlfriend's apartment. They weren't even divorced yet, and he already had a girlfriend.

Janine's face burned as she pictured what the two of them had been doing when he'd had that seizure. And just like that, she found the strength to put herself first. She held up her phone and texted her mother-in-law, *I'll be there tomorrow morning.*

With a satisfied smile, she switched off her phone and went to bed.

Contentedly Ever After

It's one of the biggest cover-ups in history that the Grimm brothers were not fairy tale writers at all, but rather part of a marketing team hired by the ruling class of Europe. Their job was to take the marriage stories of the reigning monarchs and spin them into fairy tales with a happy ending. I am here to shed light on one of those stories.

My name is Flora, better known as the miller's daughter, and this is the story of Rumpelstiltskin, minus all the lies and deceit. Let's begin with the facts.

My father indeed bragged to the king that I could spin straw into gold. He did it to elevate his own status with absolutely no concern for my well-being. I hate that jackass. It is also true that the king locked me in a bedchamber for three straight nights and told me that if I didn't spin the roomful of straw into gold, he would murder me. And finally, it is true that Rumpelstiltskin saved my life and that in desperation, I agreed to give him my firstborn child as payment for his deed.

That's where the similarities end. Rumpelstiltskin didn't spin straw into gold. We don't live in a world of magical things like the Grimm brothers would have us believe.

Rumpelstiltskin was a very rich man who brought bags of his own personal gold to give to the king in order to save my life. At the time, I didn't understand why this small hunchbacked man would do that for me, but there was a good reason.

On the fourth day, as promised, the king married me. Not because he loved me, but purely out of greed. Neither he nor my father gave a flying fig in space that I was against this marriage. So here I was, stuck with this greedy, obnoxious man whose face and personality made me gag. His halitosis was unparalleled. The king and I never shared a bedroom, though those first few weeks were a horror. He would visit me in the night, and afterward demand more gold. When I explained that my powers were used up, he never came to my bedchamber again. He rotated through a string of mistresses, and that was okay with me.

Ten months into our marriage, I gave birth to a baby boy, and he became my reason for existing. When the king tried to take the boy away from me and have him raised by the royal nannies, I knew I had to escape that toxic environment. I couldn't take a chance that Prince George would grow up to be like his father. I tried to sneak him out of the palace, but guards were watching my every move. The king considered both the prince and me to be his possessions, and I was treated like a prisoner.

Just when I was at the end of my worn and tattered rope, Rumpelstiltskin appeared and saved me for the fourth time. He returned to the palace allegedly to claim my child, his prize for saving my life. He brought with him a gold bullion, a gift for the king to ensure his entrance into the palace.

When he approached me, I began to wail, begging him not to take my son. But he calmed me down and explained he wanted to help, and I felt like I had no choice but to trust him. His plan was to announce that I had three days to guess his name, and if I failed, he would claim the child as his own. In reality, he arranged for our escape. He told me to pack a bag of necessities for George and get myself expelled from the palace.

Rumpel smuggled George out of the castle hidden in a laundry bag, and the two of them vanished as if they never existed. The king couldn't track them down. He became so enraged that he stomped his left foot so hard it crashed through the wooden floor. He then banished me from the kingdom with the decree that if I should ever try to step foot in the palace again, I would be murdered on the spot.

I was saved. With the money Rumpel gave me stashed in my petticoat, I made my escape. I bought a horse and rode to the secret location, where he waited for me with George. Together, we boarded a boat to the Americas and changed our identities.

I once asked Rumpel why he helped me. After all, I was just a poor girl, a miller's daughter with nothing to my name and a very bleak future. He had risked everything for me. His gold, his business, and his whole future.

This is what he said. He had spotted me in the marketplace and was drawn in by my beauty. When he approached me to purchase some bread, I didn't look down upon him for his ugliness but instead treated him with kindness. He fell in love.

After an arduous, months-long journey, we made it to the Americas. Rumpel had enough money left over to purchase a large plot of land, which we turned into a farm. We share our home with two dogs, fifty pigs, and two hundred cows.

Sadly, Rumpel and I could never marry because technically, I am still married to the king, but we do masquerade as husband and wife. I sometimes hear murmurings that the townsfolk call us Beauty and the Beast, and they gossip that I married Rumpel for his money. I don't care. All I care about is that George, now known as Henry, is thriving and growing up well.

Unlike the fairy tale, this story does not end in a happily ever after. I am still quite scarred from all I've been through, and I live in constant fear that one day the king will find us. I rarely leave the farm. Rumpel takes care of all the business in town and brings Henry to school. Meanwhile, I'm kept very busy taking care of the animals, cooking meals, and raising my son.

I have become quite fond of Rumpel and enjoy his company. He is a good father to Henry. I am content.

Reflections of a Magic Mirror

When Laura's mother-in-law handed her the gaudy ornate mirror, she realized she had missed her true calling. She could have been a great actress. Laura fawned over the gift, promising to go to the hardware store that day to buy the proper hanging brackets. Her husband's mother was always cranky, and Laura tried hard to stay on her good side.

The next morning, Laura faked a smile as her husband Brad hung the mirror on the bedroom wall. Brad had a complicated relationship with his mother, so Laura didn't have the heart to tell him how much she hated it. The huge, tarnished bronze frame didn't go with any of their décor.

After Brad left for work, Laura walked up to the mirror and took a good look at it. "Hideous," she groaned, her lips curling into a snarl. "It will never fit in."

As she turned to walk away, she heard a voice shout, "No, *you're* hideous!"

Laura dropped to the floor as panic set in. With her health anxiety on high alert, her first thought was that this was an auditory hallucination and the first sign of schizophrenia.

She began muttering to herself, "This is just a dream, Laura, it's just a dream…"

The mirror cleared its throat. "Nope, not a dream. I am as real as that misguided tattoo on your left shoulder." Laura's hand flew to her shoulder as the mirror continued. "I know a talking mirror is a bit of a shock, so take some time to calm down, and then we'll chat. There's no hurry. I'll be right here waiting for you."

Laura crawled into bed and pulled the covers over her head. As she contemplated the situation, she decided that if she was going insane, she might as well go all out. She threw off the blanket and shouted, "Hey, mirror, how can you be talking? You don't even have a mouth."

Suddenly, a horrible thought crossed her mind. *Wait a minute, is there a microphone hidden somewhere? Is my mother-in-law gaslighting me?*

She began frantically searching for an audio device, and when it was clear there weren't any, she looked at her reflection and whispered, "Am I crazy?"

"No, Laura," the mirror replied. "My name is Mirri, and I am a magic mirror. You know, like the one in that fairy tale. Everyone knows those fairy tales were based on truth. Anyway, as long as I'm stuck here on the wall, I might as well be of some help to you. I have nothing else to do."

"Well," asked Laura, scrunching up her forehead, "if you're such a helpful mirror, why did my mother-in-law give you away? That sounds kind of stupid."

"Oh, your mother-in-law," snapped Mirri. "I tried to help her, but you just can't help someone who doesn't want to be helped." Mirri snorted, "That witch wrapped me up in old moldy newspaper and tossed me into the basement to gather dust for twenty-five years."

"Oh, my God," said Laura. "So you sat there all that time just thinking? That must have been awful."

"It was fine. When I'm covered up, I cease to exist."

Laura furrowed her brows. "I don't understand. Are you alive? Do you have a soul?"

"I am neither alive nor not alive, but yes, I definitely have a soul."

Laura stammered, "But…but…but you're a mirror. How do you have a soul?"

"How do *you* have a soul?" asked the mirror.

"Well, I guess God implanted it in me."

"Same here," snapped Mirri.

A ringing noise interrupted their conversation. Laura looked at her phone and gasped. It was her boss. "Oh, shoot" she muttered. "I forgot to go to work." She answered the call with a coughing fit before croaking, "I'm sorry, Mr. Jackson, I won't be coming in today. I'm really sick." She ended the call with another coughing fit and a giant sneeze for good measure.

She then switched off her phone and tossed it on the bed. After a brief silence, she asked, "Mirri, you said you help people. What do you do?"

"I practice something I like to call reflective therapy. I'm going to help you stop being a doormat. I heard Brad refer to you as a fat-ass this morning. Is that okay with you?"

"Well, Brad doesn't mean anything by it. It's just his way."

"I asked if you liked it."

"No," Laura said. "I actually hate it."

"Just out of curiosity," asked Mirri, is there anything else Brad says that upsets you?"

"Well," Laura said, tears stinging her eyes, "he frequently calls me a klutz and a dummy, but the thing I really hate is when he calls me crazy. I don't think mental health issues are a joke."

"Laura," said Mirri. "We have a lot of work to do. Grab a cup of coffee and a pad of paper, and we'll sort some things out."

That night, when Brad came home from work, Laura had a nice dinner waiting for him on the table. After asking about his day,

Laura said, "Brad, we need to talk."

Brad grumbled, "Oh, that's never good. I hope it's not another one of your crazy ideas."

Laura stood up and glared at him. "I don't want you to ever call me fat-ass again. Or crazy or klutzy or dumb. I will no longer tolerate any name-calling or bullying."

Brad clenched his jaw. "What's gotten into you? Can't you take a joke?"

"It's not a joke, Brad, it's bullying. Your insults are tearing me to pieces. You make me feel worthless, and I'm beginning to hate you."

Brad jumped up and shouted, "You're acting crazy! I had a stressful day at work, and I don't need this." He grabbed his coat and stormed out of their apartment.

As he stomped down the hallway, Laura chased after him, yelling, "If you're not willing to talk about it, don't bother coming back!"

She slammed the front door and ran to her bedroom. She stared into the mirror and patted herself on the back.

"Good job, Laura," she said to her reflection. "You finally stood up for yourself." Then she collapsed onto her bed and began to sob.

Later that night, as Laura dozed on the couch, she heard the front door open. Her heart sped up as Brad walked in. His eyes were on the ground, but she could see they were red-rimmed and swollen. He sat down next to her and said, "I'm so sorry. You are right about everything. I've been behaving just like my father." He began to sniffle. "He ruined our family with his bullying, and now I'm ruining ours. He turned my mother into a mean old woman."

Laura took Brad's hand and squeezed it tightly. She put a finger to her lips and said, "Shhh."

"No, let me finish," he said. "I spent the last few hours sitting on a park bench and thinking about what you said, especially the part about hating me. When I called my brother for advice, he told me I was an idiot. He told me I was screwing up everything good in my life and that if I said one more bad thing to you, he'd help you kick me out."

"Brad," Laura said as she wrapped her arms around him, "I love you, but I need you to go to marriage counseling with me. It's not an option."

"Okay."

"And after that, maybe you'll continue in therapy to try to figure out why you behave like the man you hate most in the world."

"I'll think about it."

"Okay," said Laura. She took Brad's hand and stood up. "It's late. Let's go to bed."

Before she turned out the lights, Laura glanced into the mirror and winked. The mirror reflected her wink right back.

Metamorphosis of a
Former Beauty Queen

My name is Sarah, and this is the story of how I died.

It is a tale of a sixty-five-year-old grandmother, a former beauty queen, who made the radical decision to transform herself without considering the consequences. Please don't judge me.

My story begins the first Tuesday of October at approximately 6 a.m., when I was jolted awake by a searing pain in my back followed by lightning bolts shooting up and down my legs. After my car accident six years earlier, eight of the discs in my spine had collapsed, and the pain was agonizing. Moaning softly, I wondered how my day would go. Would I need my cane or my crutches, or would the pain be so severe I needed my wheelchair?

The first thing I did after waking up was thump Charlie on the back and beg him to stop snoring. I loved that man with all my heart, but his nightly noises could be mistaken for a jackhammer. Next, I grabbed onto the bar extending from my headboard and slowly pulled myself into a sitting position. I then reached for my giant pill box and began taking my morning medications: two for pain, one for inflammation, one for spasms, one for the constipation caused by the pain meds, and one each for anxiety and depression. I often felt like everything good in my life was slipping away, wondering how much longer I could hang on.

After swallowing my pills, I lowered myself back down and waited for the pain relievers to take effect. As I often did, I closed my eyes and revisited one of my favorite memories: the day I was a finalist in the Miss New Jersey competition; the day I danced and spun on a glittery stage until the whole audience burst into applause. I will always cherish that electrifying day and how it felt to be young and beautiful and able to turn men's heads.

As hard as I tried to continue thinking of pleasant memories, I couldn't stop my thoughts from drifting to all that I had lost. I missed teaching classes in the dance studio. Cooking dinner for my family. Helping out at the homeless shelter. I missed dancing and driving. I missed my independence. Now I had to depend on my family to help me with everything. What I missed most, though, was having the strength to hold my precious grandchildren. I was grief-stricken knowing all their memories of me would be as an invalid. I didn't want to cry, but the tears flowed anyway.

As the pain relievers began to take effect, a wonderful smell wafted into the bedroom. Charlie had gotten up and made a pot of coffee, and the aroma of the delicious brew was galvanizing me into action. I cautiously swung my legs over the side of my bed and determined it would be a crutches day. Slowly, I put on some black leggings and an oversized blue sweater. I used to love wearing stylish clothing, but now I could no longer hook a bra, so my new style was big and bulky.

After breakfast, Charlie helped me put on my shoes and finish getting ready to see my pain specialist, Dr. Stein. Charlie had taken early retirement in order to drive me to all my doctor appointments, and thinking about his sacrifice always made me sad. He used to love being a history professor.

After arriving at the doctor's office, Charlie and I sat in the waiting room scrolling through recent photos on our phones and laughing at pictures of our hilarious grandkids. I put my head on Charlie's shoulder, and he squeezed my hand, knowing how much I had been looking forward to the relief the steroid injection would bring.

We talked about Dr. Stein and how he was the kind of doctor who always took the time to listen to his patients, unlike some of my doctors, who treated me like a useless old woman. Of course, the thing that mattered most was that Dr. Stein was knowledgeable about all the latest techniques in pain management. He offered exciting experimental treatments and kept me hopeful.

When I hobbled into the examination room, I was surprised to see a second doctor there. Dr. Stein introduced me to his colleague Dr. Frank, a neurosurgeon, and said they had an exciting surprise for me. After helping me up on the examining table, Dr. Frank explained that he and Dr. Stein had discovered an experimental treatment that would alleviate my pain entirely.

I barked out, "Ha!" and told the doctors they were crazy, but they asked me to please keep an open mind.

Then an odd thing happened. The doctors presented me with a document to sign. I've signed tons of papers in doctor's offices, but this one was different. I had to vow I would never repeat what they were about to say. As I signed, my heart raced. I was equal parts nervous and excited. What an intrigue.

The doctors then approached me, lowered their voices, and told me there was a thirty-year-old in a nearby hospital who had recently suffered brain damage after a prolonged seizure. The injury was so severe the victim was about to be declared legally dead, though the body was in excellent condition.

Dr. Frank then disclosed that he had recently perfected brain transplant surgery. He could put my brain inside the thirty-year-old's head and make me young, beautiful, and healthy again. As I began screaming with excitement, Dr. Stein clapped his hand over my mouth. I felt like I was in a dream.

I crowed, "How could you conceal this remarkable discovery from the world? Why would you do that?"

Well, I guess I shouldn't have been surprised to hear the surgery had not yet been approved by the FDA; both Drs. Frank and Stein could lose their licenses if this discovery were revealed. Here's the thing—Dr. Stein knew me well. He saw how much I had been suffering and how much I had lost. He was aware of my depression and anxiety and how desperate I had become. He recognized I would be the ideal candidate for this surgery. I swore I would never report them. And I never will.

With my heart pounding like a jackhammer, I asked, "What happens to me…to my body?" Already knowing I would have to die.

The doctors told me that if I said yes, the plan would be to tell my family that Dr. Frank had pioneered a new pain-relieving surgery. That he would implant an electric stimulator in my brain that would block pain signals. After the surgery, my family would be told that I'd had a stroke and died.

Meanwhile, the brain-dead thirty-year-old would be in the same operating room. Their family would be told that Dr. Frank, as a last resort, would implant a brain stimulator to try and restore brain function. They would live, and I would die. I would wake up as a healthy thirty-year-old with nothing more than a headache. I would be reborn.

I shivered as my thoughts immediately turned to my family. I asked the doctors if I would ever be able to see them again. They barked out a vehement, "No!" The success of this project was incumbent upon it remaining a secret. Even the family of the injured person would never know the truth.

Dr. Stein recommended that I arrange to say goodbye to my family that night because the next day, I would be dead. At that point, every cell in my brain was racing at the speed of light, and I began hatching a plan of my own. It was brilliant.

My younger daughter Jessie was thirty, the age that I would soon be. I would join the yoga studio where she worked and become her friend; I already knew everything about her. She would eventually invite me to her home, where I could meet Charlie and make him fall in love with me again. For all the sacrifices Charlie made for me, he deserved to have a young, beautiful, healthy wife. It was the perfect plan.

Dr. Frank tapped me on the shoulder and shook me out of my fantasy. It was time for a decision. The accident victim's body was deteriorating rapidly, and the surgery would need to be done the next morning.

I could barely breathe, I wanted this so badly, but how could I do this to my family? I felt an overwhelming sadness for my children, but then I told myself that I was a burden to them. That I had been for years. That they would be better off without me.

I took a deep breath and blurted out, "Yes."

The doctors smiled and said, "Wonderful. We'll make all the arrangements."

That evening, my daughters and grandchildren came over for dinner, and as I looked into their beautiful faces, it broke my heart to know that they would soon be mourning their mother. Afterward, I lay awake in bed for hours, unmedicated, savoring my pain, convincing myself that the decision was justifiable.

Just before midnight, in a panic, I called my daughter Jessie. I told her that if anything happened to me during surgery, I would find a way to send her a message. "If a woman calls you on the phone and says 'fandango,' that's me. Remember that word. Fandango."

Jessie chuckled, "Okay, Mom," and we both said good night.

I woke up the next morning crying, and Charlie cuddled with me in bed until it was time to get ready. I wrestled with my decision the whole drive to the hospital, going over it again and again. When we arrived, I was put in a private room, and two nurses came in to prep me for the procedure. Charlie held my hand on the gurney as I was wheeled into surgery, and I had my last kiss ever as Sarah. Drs. Frank and Stein were already in the operating room when I got there, and I called them over and made them promise that I would wake up.

The last thing I remember as Sarah was being told to count down from ten. The next thing I knew, I was waking up in a hospital room with a massive headache. My first thought was *I am still me.*

Slowly, I opened my eyes and began to grin. I no longer had cataracts, and my back wasn't hurting. With my new crisp and clear vision, I saw Dr. Frank walking over from across the room. He bent down and whispered that the surgery had gone well. He said that my new family had been told that I had amnesia, so I wouldn't remember who they were or much else about my life. That I would have to relearn almost everything.

Meanwhile, events had transpired so quickly that I hadn't even given a thought to my new family. Apparently, I had a mom and a dad and a family that loved me. But now my thoughts were swirling again. I would have to figure out a way to dump this new family and get back together with Charlie. But that plan was for another day.

Meanwhile, in my haste to agree to the surgery, I had never questioned what my new name would be. I asked Dr. Frank who I was and nearly jumped a foot in the air when I heard my new voice.

I quickly raised my arms and saw two thick, masculine hands with a wedding ring on the fourth finger. I began hyperventilating, whimpering, "What did I do, what did I do?"

Dr. Frank gently said, "Everything will be okay. From this moment on, you are Joseph Aaron Lawrence."

I started groaning and sobbing. I didn't know how to be a man, and I didn't *want* to be a man. This had ruined all my plans.

I looked up at Dr. Frank and sniveled, "Are there any other shocking surprises?"

He smiled. "I have wonderful news. Your wife is six months pregnant. You are about to become a daddy."

I snatched Dr. Frank's phone out of his shirt pocket and began dialing my daughter Jessie's number, screaming "Fandango! Fandango!"

Dr. Frank grabbed the phone out of my hands. "Let your family mourn. You have a new daughter to think about."

I put my manly hands over my heavily bandaged head and noticed a young woman with a big belly peering in through the door. Dr. Frank beckoned to her, and she came running over and sat on my bed. She wiped the tears off my face and wrapped her arms around me, crying, "Oh, Joey, I thought I'd lost you."

I didn't know who this woman was. She was not my family. All I wanted was Charlie.

My name is Joseph, and this is the story of how I was born.

Special Thanks

Mere words on a page cannot express how much your help has meant to me. This is but a small token of my gratitude.

A giant thanks to my daughter Nicole Gerber for reading the many different versions of my stories and being my harshest critic. When you said, "Mom, I just don't like it," I knew I had to up my game.

A million thanks to my daughter Jessalyn Brower for being my second-harshest critic and my technology guru. When you're done reading this, would you mind updating my website?

Many thanks to my son Ryan Gerber for being my voice of reason in times of stress and for teaching me how to make a TikTok video.

Thank you to my husband, David Gerber, for encouraging me to publish this book even when I felt like giving up.

To Jeri Kadison, thank you for your unconditional support in all things writing, for all your helpful suggestions, and for being my very first reader.

Thank you to Marie Johnson-Ladson for keeping our writing group together during that awful pandemic and to Joe and Joan Mach for listening to my stories over and over again and always saying something nice.

Many, many thanks go to my editor, Vince Font, for correcting all my mistakes big and small, for all the helpful suggestions, and for teaching me that my grasp of the English language is not nearly as good as I thought. I couldn't have done it without you.

Thank you to Judith San Nicolas Villalonga for the beautiful cover art. I love it so much.

Thank you to my four tinys, Max, Eliana, Lev, and Hannah, for putting a smile on my face each and every day.

To my dear readers, thank you so much. Sincerely. Thank you.

–Peggy Gerber

Acknowledgments

Thanks to the editors of the following journals in which these stories have appeared (in different versions, some with different titles):

Daily Science Fiction
"Dreams Do Come True"

Reedsy
"Metamorphosis of a Former Beauty Queen"
"Angela's Super-Surprise Wedding"
"Anatomy of a Conspiracy Theory"

Terror House Magazine
"What's a Grandma"
"Squirrely Consequences"
"The Doll with the Creepy Glass Eyes"

Spillwords
"Halloween Horror House"
"Message from the Other Side"

Bewildering Stories
"The Cake with the Secret Ingredient"

The World of Myth Magazine

"The Crucial Election"
"Time-Twisted Destiny"
"The Witch in the Corner House"
"The Doll That Saved Christmas"
"A Bloody-Good Christmas Surprise"

Calliope Magazine
"The Mystical Waiting Room"

Tales of Witches and Warlocks
"My Year with the Witch"

Down in the Dirt Magazine
"Adam and Amber Escape the Planet"
"The Cake That Melted Sorrows"

Friday Flash Fiction
"True Love's Kiss"
"Inside NASA's Hidden Files"

101words.com
"Slip Click"
"What's Privacy"

50-word Stories
"Visiting Grandma"

Modern Magic
"The Mystical Rock"

Particular Passages: Autumn Breezeway
"Aunt Clarice's Bloody-Good Pumpkin Pie"

Personal Bests Journal: Volume 1
"Saving Aaron"

About the Author

Peggy Gerber is the 2021 winner of the Open Contract Challenge and the author of two poetry chapbooks, *Stumbling in CrazyTown* and *The Big Indignity*. When she's not busy writing poetry, she likes to indulge her love of speculative fiction by writing stories of time machines, friendly aliens, creepy glass dolls, and other phantasmagoria. Her works have appeared in numerous publications including *Daily Science Fiction*, *Better than Starbucks*, *Bewildering Stories*, and many anthologies. Peggy lives in Northern New Jersey with her husband, David, and enjoys reading, traveling, playing with her grandkids, and all things magical. Follow her on Instagram and Twitter @peggysue445.